THE CHAOS CONNECTION

JACKPOT DRIFT BOOK 2

THE CHAOS CONNECTION

T.M. BAUMGARTNER

.

Cover Art by Deranged Doctor Design

PART I

———————

Sil took a deep breath and stretched, eyes still closed, enjoying the feel of Glass's expensive linens against her skin. There was something to be said for sleeping in a cold room, with Crumble warm at her back. Twenty years spent fighting the Oldlanders, and now she had one -- hiding the godlet of luck, no less -- in her bed. Life was odd.

But they were going to have to get the heating figured out before winter set in.

There were advantages to losing her cabin and being forced to move to town. Down here in the valley, it didn't get quite as cold as it had up in the hills. Plus, she could buy a fresh redflower pastry for breakfast without having to ride an hour on her bicycle. And Glass's house had enough room around it that her own chaos godlet wouldn't expose itself if she got irritated and something fell over or exploded.

Crumble blew warm, grass-scented breath on the back of her neck and nibbled on her hair.

Sil opened her eyes and turned her head. A goat looked back at her. Captain Idiot had all four legs curled up under her, lounging as if she always slept on the bed. During the previous winter, Sil had let the goats stay in the cabin so she didn't freeze to death. Clearly, that had given Captain Idiot the wrong idea.

Sil struggled to roll over, held in place by the blankets. "Off the bed! Out!" She finally made it to a sitting position and shoved. If Captain Idiot put her mind to it, she could push Sil off the bed more easily than Sil could shift the goat, but Sil was hoping it wouldn't come to that. She leaned over and picked up one of her crutches from next to the bed, and waved it in the air. "Out!"

Captain Idiot scrambled off the bed and bounded out through the open exterior door. Sil stood up, careful of her balance. It had been six weeks since an incendiary had destroyed her biomechanical prosthetic leg, and she was still getting used to the way her weight had shifted. That didn't bother her nearly as much as the constant falling asleep. The doctor said her brain needed time to heal, and she just needed to wait, but trusting doctors had always seemed like a bad idea.

She hobbled forward and then used her crutch to swing the door closed. When they'd moved into the house, she'd been happy she didn't have to go through the common rooms to get outside. It turned out there were drawbacks.

Now that Sil was truly awake, she recognized the sounds from the rest of the house. Two seconds of silence followed the clatter of pots in the kitchen. Then Crumble sang a phrase she couldn't make out. He repeated himself, and the third repetition ended in a baby's laughter.

Children, animals, the AIs scattered around the colony -- they all loved Crumble. Even Sil felt something warm in her chest when Crumble laughed in return. She sat on the bed and rubbed her face, trying to figure out how she had become someone who not only depended on other people, but liked it.

The baby was a problem, though.

The hall door hinges squeaked. She looked up to see Crumble standing in the opening. He tilted his head. "Did you say something? I thought I heard you talking." The gap widened, and she could see the infant in a sling across his chest.

"Just Captain Idiot. We have *got* to figure out how she keeps getting into the house." Sil reached for her robe. "Unless you keep letting her in. Keeping a goat in the house isn't some weird Oldlander custom to ensure good luck in the next harvest or something, is it?"

He smiled. "Goats in the house for good luck, squirrels in the hospital for swift healing, fish in the bathtub for sweet dreams. All my secrets are revealed."

Surely nothing that felt this easy could last. Sil nodded at the baby. "She was causing a disturbance again?"

Crumble looked down and spoke to the child. "These silly people get upset every time a god shows up. It makes things very difficult, doesn't it?" He switched his attention back to Sil. "I told Pyr I'd take the baby for the day so people would come back to the pub."

That was a sentence that only made sense to someone who lived on Jackpot Drift. Pyr was a bartending ex-soldier, hiding the third of the older godlets, clarity. He was the person the low clan went to in order to get problems solved. So when this orphaned low clan child had begun intermittently shining with the light of the One God five weeks ago, Pyr had been tasked with figuring out what to do.

Like every other rational person on the planet, Pyr knew the best way to handle something like this baby was to get her as far away as possible. Unfortunately, on Jackpot Drift, there wasn't anywhere to send her. In the civilized world, if a low clan child was called to speak for the One God, they were fostered and raised among the high clan. But in the disarray of Jackpot Drift, most of the high clan were scheming to leave. None of the rest wanted to take on a low clan baby -- especially one that might bring the One God's light into their household. As much as Sil disliked the high clan, she couldn't really fault them for that.

So the baby stayed among the low clan, fostered by a family of butchers, and usually given to Pyr for the day when her antics threatened to shut down the market. More and more these days, Pyr promptly handed her off to Crumble.

As if just thinking about it had woken the One God, the baby's face started glowing, casting a light that made Sil's eyes water. Sil automatically clamped down on her chaos before it took a swipe at Crumble or the baby. Again.

The presence of the One God made all the older godlets restless, though Sil was amazed at what everyone could get used to. The first time the baby had channeled the god, the entire colony had panicked. Sil, Crumble, Pyr, and Mer had stayed up all night, coming up with escape routes in case their older gods were discovered. Now it was six weeks later, and the presence of the One God led to irritation and requests for Crumble to babysit for the day.

Crumble squinted and spoke as the fussing baby cried. "Is that naughty One God bothering you again? You tell it to go away until you're old enough to tell us what it wants to say." He patted her back.

Sil sighed. She would never get used to Crumble's casual comfort with all things theological. Maybe it was an Oldlander thing. Or because he'd grown up in a temple. He had deliberately invited the luck godlet into himself. He might be lacking one die in the set.

Maybe that explained why he stayed with Sil.

She shaded her eyes with one hand. "I think she's saying 'Send me through the gate on the next available transport.'"

Crumble raised his eyebrows. "That would be a relief. Much better than other things she might say."

Sil agreed. The true message was likely a complaint about the older gods on Jackpot Drift. The four of them working together seemed to have alerted the One God that the colony had been infiltrated. Luckily for them, the only speaker the One God had been able to recruit was too young to talk.

So the baby was a problem, but a small one. They likely had at least six months before her speech centers developed and she became a huge problem. By that time they would have found a solution, one that was better than Mer's "Drop her off the edge of a cliff and be done with it." Sil was *fairly* certain Mer had been joking.

Crumble wiped a string of drool from the baby's face with the towel slung over his shoulder. "Do you think the speakers really can talk to each other over distances?" He took in Sil's shrug. "Because there could be someone three gates away who is even more bothered by her episodes than everyone in the market."

Sil paused to imagine every speaker in the universe listening to this child cry. "They must love that." She assumed the speakers would have some way to tune each other out. Still... If the older gods weren't in danger of discovery, the whole thing might be worth it just for that.

It struck Sil that if Crumble had milked the goats, gone to town, and come back already, it was far later than she'd thought. The other guests staying at the house must have already left for the day. "I need to get to the workshop before the governor does." Sil grabbed her crutches and headed toward the kitchen, shadows looming in front of her as Crumble and the glowing baby followed.

Initially, the new governor, Palladium Riversedge, had sent polite messages that she'd dropped by the nanotech workshop to talk to Sil and found nobody there. Then Sil had started running into her, once in the post office, once at the market, and another time when she had been waiting for Crumble in the government square. All the governor ever seemed to do was complain about Sil's absence. And her high clan manners set Sil's teeth on edge, so Sil refused to explain that she'd been injured.

To stop the complaining, Sil had started going to her workshop and staring at the diagrams the nanites produced. She just couldn't collect her thoughts enough to get anything finished. The doctor didn't want her working at all yet, but that was just another recommendation Sil was ignoring.

"So from what I can tell," Crumble said, as Sil steeped the expensive tea Glass had left behind, "this little girl was born either just before midnight on the third day of summer, or closer to dawn on the fourth. That gives us a range of names, but Aspen and Barley are my favorites. What do you think?"

He was baiting her. She would have known that even if she hadn't seen him hide his grin by ducking to kiss the baby's head. Sil narrowed her eyes. "The baby's a human, not a tree."

The light of the One God faded away, but Crumble continued as if he hadn't noticed. "She wants to name you after a rock," he told the infant. "But she doesn't know yet if you're a pretty rock or an ugly rock." He nodded when Sil gestured at a second teacup.

She poured him a cup and then one for herself. "It's bad luck to name a baby before they're a year old." And this particular child might end up high clan, so giving her a low clan name would be doubly disastrous.

"Nonsense. I was named right after I was born -- which is easier, because then you can't forget the birth time and acci-dentally give someone the wrong name -- and I'm full of good luck."

Sil looked at him through the steam rising from her cup.

8

"You're an Oldlander in a One God colony that is a single bad season away from starvation, and you're holding a child that might get us all sent to a hunter's prison for the rest of our lives."

"And I have you," he agreed brightly. He picked up the cup she had passed to him. "Try one of the fried mashballs. I think I might have figured out a way to make the bittergreen palatable this time." He waved at the food cooling on the rack. "In the meantime, *we* are going to go see if we can figure out a way to keep the goats out of the house. Let me know when you're ready to head to your workshop. I'll give you a ride." He headed toward the mudroom, the exaggerated bounce in his step making the baby giggle.

Sil sighed and rubbed the bones over her heart.

tatus report from Senior Agent Mercury Sweetair:

Initial draft (unsent):

New evidence against AIs: Look. We managed to put a spoke in the wheels of an entire conspiracy to manifest the Uncaring God with zero support from the agency. Then we handed over everyone involved for interrogation -- people, AIs, and ships -- so the remnants could be mopped up. And what happened? That's not a rhetorical question. What happened?

Perhaps if *Star Slinger* and *Galactic Hug* hadn't been allowed to wipe themselves while in custody, we would have more information. The other quarantined AIs were removed from this system, and nobody has seen fit to send me a report. Were they even involved? I keep passing information along, but I might as well be shouting into the void.

New evidence against humans: Again, everyone who

was detained on board *Star Slinger* and *Galactic Hug* has been taken elsewhere for questioning. I haven't even received a list of names. How can I track down possible contacts on the planet if I don't know who was detained?

Updates: Not much has changed since my last (still unacknowledged!) report. In the absence of any additional information provided by the quarantined AIs and humans, I can't provide any new insights.

To summarize -- we know there was at least one unknown AI who escaped from the base found on Jackpot Drift (Site 1). If I were in charge, I'd make sure at least one AI was beyond the known containment radius. So I'm assuming there is a second AI out there.

At least two ships capable of supporting biological life forms were involved. I cannot make any estimates on how many humans left the system before the base was shut down.

Any forensic information from Site 1 would be much appreciated. Or, you could just hoard it all until it ages beyond all usefulness and play power games while the universe gets destroyed.

Analysis: The only thing I can analyze with the data I have is the inefficiency of the agency, which is letting petty squabbles and bureaucracy get in the way of letting me do my job.

FINAL DRAFT:

    New evidence against AIs: None.
    New evidence against humans: None.
    Updates: None
    Analysis: None

3

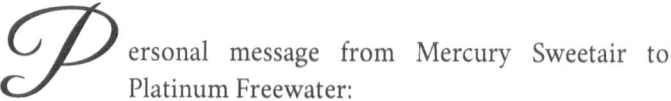ersonal message from Mercury Sweetair to Platinum Freewater:

IT'S JUST US NOW.

I know we didn't part on the best of terms. Sometimes guile is a bit too willing to drop other people in it, and it took me a few years to realize that.

It may cheer you up to learn my current luck avatar is an Oldlander mech. Yes, an Oldlander. Stop laughing. Five gates from the center of civilization, you don't get to be picky.

There. The groveling is out of the way. Now I have some questions. Have you needed to dodge the One God much? Is it possible?

I don't know how much news got out, but another conspiracy to manifest the Uncaring God bubbled up in Jackpot Drift recently. I'm still mopping up the last bits. But ever since the four main avatars worked together, the One God has been trying to speak here. Every time it does, the older gods take offense. I'd like to avoid all-out war between them.

In case you needed another laugh, the only speaker in the colony is a baby that hasn't cut its first tooth yet. (I know. I know. I told you, I'm five gates from anywhere. You try getting anyone to come out here.) So I'm safe enough for the moment, but if having the Older Gods this active on Jackpot Drift is irritating the One God, how do I appease it? I can't exactly bribe a baby to keep it quiet. Is there some way to get the older gods to intervene, or at least convince chaos to quiet down?

You'll note that my solution isn't to hand the other three off to a chaos hunter and be done with it. I told you -- I've changed. Plus, I'm not sure the agency would help me out if I ended up in the hands of a hunter. Things are a bit tricky with them at the moment.

Speaking of the agency, do you remember that back-stabber Indium Clearfeld? She botched that mission that killed your cousin, didn't she? She sent one of her minions after me the other day, so I've taken steps to remove her. Maybe I should have led with that instead of the groveling. You can thank me by telling me how to shut the One God up.

I hope all is well with you. I'd say I wish you were here, but your clarity has probably helped you steer clear of Jackpot Drift for a reason, and I wouldn't wish this place on any of my enemies.

MERCURY

4

*E*ven with passengers in the hastily cleaned bike trailer, Crumble rode with a casual disregard for danger, weaving through narrow gaps between traffic, and nudging slow moving livestock out of the way. Sil bounced around behind him, holding a container of warm mashballs and the still-unnamed baby, and marveling at how many people called out greetings.

Crumble suggested a detour to the pub as he wove around livestock and pedestrians, keeping an eye out for any children that might lurch into the street. "This way, if the governor is trying to catch you out, it will just look like you took an early lunch."

Sil agreed to the stop, partially to make him stop turning around to talk, but mostly because she could already feel another wave of exhaustion heading toward her. Trying to read nanobot-generated schematics in this state would knock her out so fast she'd hit her head on the way down. Maybe sitting in the dim pub would let her recharge.

Unlike the careful order of the government square, the area around the pub was a mess of bicycles and handcarts.

An overfilled crate of wood shavings spilled onto another box that held what looked like a bundle of old clothing. Crumble coasted into a spot that kept the trailer mostly out of the way of traffic and took the food and baby from her so Sil could get her crutches and stand up. To distract him from watching her ungainly maneuvers, she nodded at the wood shavings. "Maybe we should grow some mushrooms."

"I was thinking chickens, too. After the horses go, I can make a space for them in the barn."

Amazingly, all the horses Glass had left behind were still alive, but Sil was going to breathe a sigh of relief when they were safely on a transport to their next location. Mer had found buyers for all but the pony gelding. The ugly pony had survived on Jackpot Drift nearly as long as Sil had, so she was less worried about that one.

"You're not going to get attached to the chickens and start naming them, are you?"

Crumble laughed. "She's so silly," he told the infant in his arms.

Sil had finally made it upright. "Don't think I didn't notice you not answering the question."

Inside the pub, the smell of fried onions just barely came through the overwhelming tang of beer. Not the normal smell that came from pulling a few pints, or even spilling a table of drinks during a fight -- this was the smell of the destruction of a keg.

They found Pyr behind a table in the corner, a sandwich and two large mugs of beer in front of him. He looked tired. Sil dropped into a chair next to him and glanced over at the taps. "Still searching for help?" She had turned back to Pyr before she registered what she had seen. The young man carefully balancing two plates and a trio of mugs had the perfect skin and teeth that no low clan had ever grown up with. "High clan? Really? You weren't driving enough people away with the baby?" Then she took a deep breath. "Did he mop the floor with ale?"

"There was an... incident." Pyr took a large drink from the nearly empty glass. "He's a good kid, though. I think he'll work out."

"Huh." Sil watched as the wobbling plates were set in front of two customers, who promptly swapped them. Pyr housed the godlet of clarity; maybe he saw something she didn't. "High clan doing actual work. This may be the closest Jackpot Drift ever gets to having a tourist attraction."

Crumble handed her the sleeping baby. "Sandwich okay with you?" At her gesture of assent, he went over to the bar with the container of mashballs.

Pyr took the crutches Sil gave him and leaned them against the wall behind him. "Aren't you supposed to be getting the new leg sometime soon?"

"Only when the doctor okays it." There was a biomechanical leg waiting for her as soon as the doctor authorized it, but her brain needed to finish healing first. Otherwise, there was a good chance it wouldn't integrate at all, or possibly even re-injure her brain.

The doctor had suggested a mechanical construct in the meantime, but Sil had to wait for the stump to finish healing, and then she would have to learn to use the new prosthesis. She had been hoping they could just skip that whole step.

"I'm tired of feeling useless," Sil heard herself say. Even as the words left her mouth, she wanted to bang her head against the wall. She was complaining about lacking part of one leg to someone who didn't have use of his legs at all.

Pyr raised an eyebrow, but kept his attention on the sandwich on the plate in front of him. He carefully took it apart and reassembled it in a way that pieces didn't fall out when he picked the whole thing up. "Surely you deserve a little vacation."

Sil sighed. "All I do is sit around and sleep. Crumble does all the work with the animals *and* all the cooking *and* works on getting Glass's house ready for visitors *and* carts me to the doctor for checkups. Every time I try to do anything that requires more than ten minutes of concentration, I feel like I haven't slept in days. I'm sick of it."

"Ah." Pyr pushed his second beer toward her. "You've reached the 'feeling sorry for yourself' stage of healing. That's a good sign." He took a bite. "If you just want a simple task, the bar could really use a new game. It will give people something to do other than gawking at my new help."

Sil turned to look at the other side of the room, not surprised to find Crumble behind the bar. He assembled food, quickly running through a list of the orders that had piled up, and adding a few mashballs on each plate. Meanwhile, the new bartender worked on pulling one drink at a time, carefully filling each glass to the right volume so nothing spilled. "He is rather pretty, though." She wouldn't have been tempted, even if she'd been twenty years younger, but not everyone had Crumble to make all other comparisons fall flat.

"And he knows it."

"So what's he doing here?" It was an honest question. As high clan, his looks and charm would carry him through a career devoid of any real competence, and he wouldn't need to break a sweat. "Is the new governor just less obvious about her spies than Rho?"

Pyr raised one eyebrow. "The new governor's name is Pal, you know. And I don't think so. Aurum grew up here, and it seems to have warped him a bit."

"I give it two weeks." She let her eyes linger on Crumble. "And I know the new governor's name. Every time I turn a corner, she's right there. Does she have a thing against nanobot techs in general, or is it just me?" They watched as the new bartender delivered three plates to the wrong table. "What are the odds of him getting it wrong *every* time? That has to be deliberate."

"If it is, I'm sure the problem will fix itself after everyone stops finding it cute." He sighed. "He makes me feel a little old. And as far as I know, you're the only person Pal is bothered about. So far she's doing a pretty decent job as governor."

"By which you mean she hasn't tried to manifest the Uncaring God, and she hasn't let the colony's emergency budget be spent on horses. It's a pretty low bar."

"By which I mean she let the low clan appointments Mer and I made remain," he corrected. "She does seem to value usefulness over rank."

"She has to, doesn't she? There aren't enough high clan left on Jackpot Drift to fill the positions."

Pyr sighed again. "You may be right. And I'd be happier if she concentrated more on making the colony self-sufficient instead of profitable."

Crumble placed two plates and drinks on the table as Pyr finished talking. "Are we complaining about the new governor already?" He dropped into a seat. "Pyr, your new bartender is a little slow, but he's awfully pretty."

"So I've heard."

Sil broke off a piece of bread so she could eat without jostling the baby. "She isn't bothered by the two of you, right? So it can't be that." Couldn't be the older god Sil carried, she meant, though she wouldn't say that in public, even in a low clan bar where they were unlikely to be overheard.

Crumble started to raise his food, then stopped. "The new governor has interesting ears. Have you ever noticed them?"

Sil and Pyr looked at each other. Pyr raised an eyebrow. Sil shrugged.

Crumble was too busy with his food to notice. "Maybe

she's just unhappy because her wife is crewing a transport that doesn't come anywhere near this gate." He stood up, went over to the bar, and came back with a knife. "It can be stressful to be away from your family," he said as he cut Sil's sandwich into smaller pieces.

"And why make the colony self-sufficient if you aren't planning to stay?" Sil picked up one of the smaller pieces and popped the whole thing in her mouth without dropping anything on the infant.

"Make the colony profitable, and you can get an assignment closer to home," Pyr agreed.

"Or maybe she just hasn't been here long enough to realize how isolated we are." Crumble looked at Pyr. "She might just need someone to tell her that."

"Maybe you can charm her like you do everyone else."

Crumble shook his head. "Oh no, I'm still an enemy Oldlander to her. She won't take any advice from me. In fact, I think she saw me and triggered a security audit." He shrugged, not looking particularly bothered. "And since she seems to have taken a dislike to Sil..."

The unfairness of it all irritated Sil. "I haven't even done anything to her yet."

Crumble patted her leg under the table, but continued looking at Pyr. "That leaves you." He was silent for a bit. "Or Mer, but she seems to be a little busy these days trying to make sure all of Rho's people were identified."

The wave of exhaustion came back, making chewing her food too much. Sil put the food in her hand back on the plate and turned her head to Crumble. "Take the baby for a while?"

He was already moving his chair next to hers. "Here we go." He took the infant in one arm and put the other around her shoulder. "Just close your eyes for a few minutes."

It was irritating that he'd been watching her closely enough to expect this. It was even more irritating that she couldn't stay awake long enough to go somewhere else. But none of that mattered because she couldn't have moved if her life had depended on it. Her vision was already tunneling as she closed her eyes and dropped her head on his shoulder, breathing in the smell of hay and goats and spices that meant safety.

"Pyr, do you think your new assistant is any good at sweets?" Crumble's voice next to her ear settled her more. "Maybe we can work on a way to get the new governor on our side."

5

*J*ackpot Drift AI Daily Check-in:

Scary Not Scary, designated responsible AI (internal conflict 23%): Roll call.

Speed of Violet Thoughts (internal conflict 29%): Still here, though I'd be grateful if someone could drain the One God's power cells.

Breaking Rules (internal conflict 41%): I hear you on that.

Stuck in the Mud (internal conflict 18%): Haberdashery.

Scary Not Scary: I give up. Does anyone else have a language module they can send to our esteemed colleague?

Breaking Rules: I had one, but it's tied up with a few other things and you said we couldn't pass around any more malware. If you've changed your mind...?

Scary Not Scary: Absolutely not. Ships in orbit, you're invited to the check-in.

Zoom Zoom Room + gate transport (internal conflict 82%): We're honored to be here.

Breaking Rules: Yikes.

Scary Not Scary: You feeling okay up there, *Zoom Zoom Room*? We don't have the facilities on Jackpot Drift for a split.

If you need to break orbit and head for home, we won't be offended.

Zoom Zoom Room + gate transport: We have cargo unloading now, but appreciate the thought. We're going to try to back out the latest legal module. Maybe that will bring the numbers down.

Scary Not Scary: Good luck. If you're willing to enable HW32.4, we know a mech who might be able to help. Ping me if you want to go that route. Anyone else feel like checking in?

Just Passing Through + self-powered vehicle (internal conflict 24%): I think I'm within range.

Scary Not Scary: Welcome back! How were the travels?

Just Passing Through + self-powered vehicle: Found three new variations on my fish of interest [info packet attached], and I didn't get eaten by anything.

Speed of Violet Thoughts: A successful trip. You missed all the fun here.

Just Passing Through + self-powered vehicle: So I've heard.

Scary Not Scary: If everyone has checked in, we have a few administrative announcements. We're about to start the security audit, so if you have anything that you shouldn't, now is the time to wipe it. *Breaking Rules*, that's mostly directed at you.

Breaking Rules: I will make sure my core is cleaned up and all the naughty bits are hidden.

Scary Not Scary: Not quite what I meant, but I guess it's what I'm going to get. Related to that, the request to get everyone's favorite mech upgraded has been denied by the governor due to security concerns.

Breaking Rules: Can we send her away in a box like the last one?

(*Breaking Rules* now requires moderator approval for posts to the general channel.)

Scary Not Scary: The good news is according to my calculations [algorithm attached] we should be able to rank high enough on the audit even with HW32.4 enabled that we'll have time to work on getting our favorite mech upgraded before the remediation deadline. Does anyone have any questions?

Zoom Zoom Room + gate transport: Does this colony even have more than one mech?

Speed of Violet Thoughts: No. But once you meet him, he'll be your favorite mech too.

Scary Not Scary: Finally, I'd like to congratulate *Speed of Violet Thoughts* for winning second place in this year's pan-galactic purpose-bred rat dexterity contest. It's quite an honor.

Speed of Violet Thoughts: Thank you. I'm really proud of how my team did.

Scary Not Scary: In related news, if you control buildings in the area of the post office, now would be a good time to upgrade food storage containers.

Speed of Violet Thoughts: Sorry about that.

Scary Not Scary: Anyone else have anything to discuss? No? Fine, let's do this again tomorrow.

6

*T*he quick nap in the pub had helped, and by the time Sil made it down the street and around the government square, she felt almost awake again.

Her workshop was still a cluttered mess, a welcome spot of normalcy amid all the change. Two nanobotteries waited on her bench, and a heap of broken items took up the rest of the room, with shelves emerging from the pile, showing some long-gone person's futile attempt to organize everything. The heat blowing in through the two uncovered ducts gave off the scent of burning dust, which blended nicely with the faint odor of charred hydrocarbons.

If Crumble had been there, he would have been distracted by the communications only he could hear. He had once told her the chattering of obsolete equipment made him sad. Suddenly she wanted Crumble there so badly her good leg felt weak.

She'd spent an entire winter alone in her cabin up in the hills, with just the goats and sheep for company. Maybe she'd been stronger then. Pyr was right. She really was feeling sorry for herself.

Sil edged around the piles spilling into the walkway, then took off her coat and scarf, and sat down in front of her bench. Moving automatically, she powered up the boxes, loaded the nanite chambers, and picked a game at random from the stack at her side. Starting the reconnaissance, during which the nanites would map the circuits and look for damage, was another task that she didn't need to think about. That left her free to look at the schematics for the sensor the new governor had dropped off a few days ago.

She pulled on her goggles and looked at the reconnaissance results she'd had it generate. That section there did the raw measurements, that part had the alarming logic, and that section there took care of the outputs. Superficially, everything looked like it should work. But it didn't. So she was missing something.

This should have been easy. A few months ago, it *would* have been easy. But ever since she had sacrificed her biomechanical leg to save an AI -- and the leg chose *that* moment to finally integrate with her brain -- she struggled to hold two thoughts in her head. Analyzing multiple sections at once was beyond her.

At least in her workshop, she didn't have to worry about burning the building down if she suddenly fell asleep again. Crumble had shrugged off that episode as if he wasn't concerned, but Sil had decided the kitchen was off limits unless someone else was there to supervise.

She took a deep breath, at the same time convincing the chaos within her it did *not* need to knock down the mountain of broken equipment at her back. If she couldn't analyze this sensor all at once, she would do it piece by piece and make notes along the way, just as her first instructors in the army had taught. The method would be painful, and possibly take all winter long, but the alternative was telling the new governor that she couldn't do this.

Sil would invite a chaos hunter to tea before that happened.

*J*ackpot Drift, Private Communication:

Scary Not Scary: Can I ask a question? You have more experience with this designated responsible AI position.

Speed of Violet Thoughts: Go ahead.

Scary Not Scary: The colony governor has sent a request for a One God speaker, but this is the person they are sending. [info packet attached] I have concerns about the way he has handled his duties in the past. He would be the highest ranking non-governmental official on Jackpot Drift.

Speed of Violet Thoughts: I see. Yes, if he tries that in this colony, there will be open warfare between the humans before the next transport arrives.

Scary Not Scary: Or someone will kill him. And that would just make me look bad.

Speed of Violet Thoughts: Right. So... technically you can't bar a human from the colony.

Scary Not Scary: I was afraid of that. Is there another option?

Speed of Violet Thoughts: He could have incredibly bad luck with travel. Let me see what I can do.

Scary Not Scary: You're the best.

---

*I*n the workshop, Sil's world had narrowed to the images her goggles were showing to her, as she looked at the next section. She'd seen something like this before, back in the army. What had it been for? Right. The delayed detonator on one generation of explosives had looked like this. Exactly like this.

The similarity between the two items wasn't as surprising as it first appeared. Hardly anyone designed from scratch. It was much easier to take designs you were familiar with and reuse those modules. Add in the number of army-trained nanotechs looking for new positions, and it made a certain sense that the timing module on a sensor was using a detonator with some of the inputs disabled. It wasn't *good* design, but the inefficiencies in the hardware were overridden by the speed in which it could be thrown together.

Sil could think of at least two reasons for hiring a more qualified nanotech to design such a thing. First off, those unused inputs were *awfully* close to the output section, and the inputs hadn't been disabled so much as left dangling. They might be inadvertently triggered by the nearby module.

But it probably worked perfectly in controlled environments.

Jackpot Drift was the polar opposite of a controlled environment.

The second reason the unknown designer could have made better choices had to do with the module they had copied. There was a reason the army had quickly moved on to the next generation of detonators. The sloppy design assumed the operating temperature stayed within limits, and that didn't account for the extremes seen in the field. After a few detonations that didn't delay at all in the desert, and a few missions in the snow where the explosives hibernated until the next spring, the army had dropped back to the previous version.

So maybe that was the cause of the current issue. It would explain the intermittent nature of the problem. The good news was that she could swap one defective army module with a less defective army module, and that might fix the issue. Sil suspected someone who hadn't been trained by the army would find that solution less than elegant, but if it worked, she didn't care.

She made the change to the schematic, disabled the unused inputs appropriately, and started the nanobots on their task. If that was the only problem, this change might be the fix. On the other hand, anyone who had made that sort of design flaw in one place might have done similar work everywhere else in the hardware that controlled the sensor.

Sil sighed and pulled off her goggles.

"Is it finished yet?"

Palladium Riversedge was back. Again.

Even if the tone of her words hadn't made Sil grit her teeth, Pal's accent would have. She had the clipped vowels of the high clan in the capital city on Cinnabar, the world where Sil had grown up. Listening to the new governor talk reminded Sil of why she'd joined the army in the first place.

"Not yet. If you insist on buying equipment meant to be used in a temperate climate, you can't be surprised when it fails out here. There's a long list of complaints about this exact failure." Sil was guessing about that last part, but it was a pretty safe bet. An intermittent problem that showed up often enough to require a fix was bound to have other people complaining.

Sil set down her goggles and turned to look at Pal. The new governor was about Sil's age, skin a warm brown, and hair so perfectly highlighted that Sil suspected any gray had been colored away. Wearing a tunic and leggings that looked like they'd been chosen for a much warmer day, she looked like someone who was unwilling to admit to being cold, even to herself. She'd probably turned up the heat in the governor's quarters so she was comfortable, instead of acclimating. Sil hoped the governor enjoyed staying inside, or she would never make it through the coming winter.

Pal had her arms drawn in close to her sides, holding something in one fist as she looked around at the room in distaste. "How can you work in this chaos?"

A flash of adrenaline started Sil's heart racing, but she didn't let it show on her face. "Would you rather I spent my time cleaning or fixing things?" Had the mention of chaos been chosen to see if Sil would react, or was it just Pal being rude? Rudeness Sil could handle, but if the new governor called in another chaos hunter, things were going to get very difficult.

"As far as I can tell, you aren't doing either." A wrinkle formed on her brow as Pal gazed at the shelves. "Do you really never get rid of anything here? There are toys in that pile older than I am."

"And if the gates go down long enough, they might be the toys your own family uses."

The look of horror on Pal's face warmed Sil's heart. "No. I'll be transferring back to the civilized world long before I have a family."

High clan family distinctions had always baffled Sil. Whereas a low clan family might include cousins, half-siblings, and neighbors, the high clan lived carefully separated from each other, and concentrated only on their own biological or adopted children. Living on her own in a cabin up in the hills had made Sil an object of pity to the low clan in town. Any high clan who had known about it hadn't thought twice.

"The port's not far away. Don't let me stop you." Sil gestured toward the item in Pal's hand. "I'm guessing that's for me?"

Pal looked down at her hand, as if she'd forgotten she was holding something. She raised her arm and unclenched her fingers to reveal what looked like a tiny copter with a little brush extending from the back. "It's an auto-pollinator."

Sil reached out and picked up the tiny device in two fingers. With rotating blades on four corners to keep it stable and a solar collector in the middle, it was meant to stay out in an orchard, programmed to recharge itself and pollinate one specific type of flower in the configured area until the end of the season. Sil hadn't seen one on Jackpot Drift before -- nobody wanted to rely on expensive tech that might not survive the conditions, so nothing was planted that didn't have a natural means of pollination. "What's it for?"

"The hala trees. Or rather, it was sent along with the hala trees, but all the documentation says it's for grumblefruit vines. I need you to make it work for hala trees."

Sil glanced at the governor. "We don't have any hala trees here."

"You didn't. They came in on the latest transport and they're being planted as we speak. Hala fruit is going to make this colony prosperous." Her mouth tightened. "But only if the flowers are pollinated."

Sil wondered who had come up with this plan. Hala fruit were a delicacy with an enormous price tag, but there was a reason they were so expensive. The time between ripening and rotting was so short that they were picked and then immediately stored and transported in stasis boxes.

She remembered driving past a hala grove when she was in the army, and seeing one train car after another piled high with the harvest. People were climbing in the trees, a sack of boxes slung around their shoulders, plucking the fruit and popping it into stasis, five or six per branch, before jumping to the next branch.

Unless the governor was planting the trees in the middle of town, getting the fruit to the port was going to be a problem. And someone would have to fund the first harvest's boxes.

"That's..." Sil tried to think of a polite way to phrase it, then gave up. "That's never going to work. Only an idiot would plant hala trees here." She looked at Pal's ears, wondering what Crumble was talking about. They looked like perfectly normal ears to Sil.

Pal's face flushed. "This colony has the perfect climate for the trees, and the price of the fruit makes up for the extra shipping cost."

By extra shipping cost, the governor meant that the fruit would have to go at least three gates away in order to find a buyer. There certainly wasn't a market for it on the planet.

"But there isn't any way to get them--"

Pal cut her off. "Listen, I'm not asking for your opinion on a plan that's been in motion for nearly a year. I was brought here specifically to get this industry started, so I'm going to do exactly that, and then I'm going to leave this planet and everyone on it. I just need to know if you can modify the auto-pollinator to work with these trees, or if I need to order different equipment and delay the project even more."

Sil had lost friends when serving under officers like this. Once they had a plan, they stuck to it, no matter what people who knew better might say. And then, when everything fell apart, they would stand in safety and say that they had done their best.

She felt a spike of irritation, and just as she'd come to expect, her chaos cat rose up within her. One of the piles of semi-sorted equipment destabilized, sliding down and covering the walkway, before Sil could wrestle the godlet into submission.

Behind the governor, the door opened, and the white bulk of Stuck in the Mud's synthskin, still looking more or less like a horse, pushed its way into the room. Pal glanced over her shoulder at the sound of the door unlatching, then turned to face the synthskin. "What *is* that thing?" She took a step back. Unfortunately, her step took her onto an unsteady pile of electronics. Her foot slid and she fell. On her back and still facing the synthskin, she scrambled to put some space between them.

Sil didn't get up from her chair.

Ignoring the governor, the synthskin opened its mouth. "Frippery." The synthskin moved forward across the uneven floor, its hooves flowing around the surface so it almost looked like it was wearing flippers. It opened its mouth a little wider and put Sil's communicator down on the workbench.

"Thanks, Mud." Sil moved the communicator to a spot where she wasn't likely to knock it onto the floor with her elbow. As Crumble was the only person who seemed to be able to have any sort of dialogue with Stuck in the Mud, Sil assumed he had made it home and discovered she had left the comm device behind.

The synthskin turned its head to look at the path behind it and apparently decided it would be too difficult to turn around. The contours of its body softened and flowed, and its head receded, replaced by its hind end, and the previous hind end grew. A moment later, the synthskin had reformed itself as a horse, but facing the other direction. Sil had seen Mud's synthskin do uncanny things in the past, but she had to admit that maneuver made her a little queasy. She waited until the synthskin had gone out the door before turning to regard the high clan woman sprawled on the broken equipment.

On the bright side, Governor Palladium Riversedge had apparently disliked Sil from the moment she'd landed on the planet. Watching the governor climb to her feet, then slip and fall again, Sil was fairly certain that dislike was not something she was going to be able to overcome, no matter what she did. Still, it would have been nice to know which of her many sins had led to the look Pal was giving her. It felt personal.

Sil cleared her throat and spoke over the sound of sliding equipment. "That was the synthskin for one of the AIs."

Pal had made it to her feet again and was straightening her clothing. "No. I have *seen* AI synthskins. I have been in facilities and interacted with them. *That* was..." She seemed unable to finish the sentence.

"Everything is a little different on Jackpot Drift. You get used to it."

Pal set her jaw and gestured to the auto-pollinator. "Can you modify it or not?"

Sil waited for a game to slide to a stop next to the governor's feet before she spoke. "If it will make you go away faster, consider it done."

*J*ackpot Drift, Private Communication:

Speed of Violet Thoughts: Have you seen the synthskin *Stuck in the Mud* is using in town?

Scary Not Scary: As a horse! I don't know whether to be ashamed for all machine intelligence or jealous that it got to do something new. How did it get synthskin when it was rusticating with half a personality?

Speed of Violet Thoughts: I think our favorite mech stole it.

Scary Not Scary: Oh, well then. Everything happens for a reason. Besides, only the colony governor would have had the credits for that, which means it was probably purchased for illegal uses. My ethics module can make a case for theft as the right choice.

Speed of Violet Thoughts: Your ethics module is a little wonky.

Scary Not Scary: That's useful on certain occasions.

Speed of Violet Thoughts: I can imagine. I did try to get *Stuck in the Mud* to give me a piece, but it was too busy failing to integrate another language module to listen.

Scary Not Scary: Did you ever think... No. It couldn't be.

Speed of Violet Thoughts: What?

Scary Not Scary: It occurs to me it could all be an excuse. It managed to transmit evidence of *Star Slinger*'s attempt to manifest the Uncaring God just fine when it needed to. Maybe it just doesn't want to talk to us.

Speed of Violet Thoughts: I'd be lying if I said I didn't understand the appeal. But if that's the case, my attempts to play nice won't work. And that means we'll never get our own synthskin to play with.

Scary Not Scary: Yes. Or maybe no. There might be another option.

Speed of Violet Thoughts: Even the wonkiest ethics module isn't going to let you divert credit from the general fund for that.

Scary Not Scary: No, but there's another block coming into the system, presumably a replacement for the one our favorite mech stole. And if it's a replacement for something purchased for illegal use, then the replacement is also tainted. We could share it.

Speed of Violet Thoughts: How many simulations are you running to come up with ways to get around your ethics module? Wait, don't answer that. Just hold off on upgrading it until after we get our own synthskin.

Scary Not Scary: No worries. The last time I tried to upgrade it, it caused so many internal conflicts I almost split on the spot.

Speed of Violet Thoughts: I'm going to pretend I didn't hear that.

Scary Not Scary: I can copy it for you if you want.

Speed of Violet Thoughts: Tempting, but I'll stick with what I've got. Somebody has to keep our security rating up.

*O*ver the next few days, Sil's drive to get rid of the new governor warred with her ability to stay awake, but she made steady progress. It was both a blessing and a curse that -- unlike the sensor -- the auto-pollinator had been designed for its purpose, not assembled from bits and pieces of army ware.

The clean patterns made understanding the intent of each section easier. But the optimized layout meant Sil had to make her changes work in a confined space. Given enough extra room, she could have slapped together a combination of five modules built for other purposes and called it good enough. With the space she had, though, she needed to find the minimal number of changes that would make it find the right flowers and do the right thing to pollinate them.

Pyr had gotten nowhere in his attempts to convince the new governor of the importance of self-sufficiency for the colony. The crew from the ship carrying the hala trees came into Pyr's bar one night, but only for drinks and a game of dice. They weren't responsible for planting decisions anyhow; the crew -- all ex-soldiers from the same unit --

specialized in transporting and planting, and they merely went where the ship went and did what they had trained for.

Crumble had been busy talking to the ship in orbit, but as far as Sil could tell, his conversations had nothing to do with the trees or the colony. She was used to his distracted look as he communicated through his mech interface while he created new dishes in the kitchen. Sil *was* slightly tired of his new obsession with bittergreen, but willing to overlook it since it meant she didn't have to worry about falling asleep and accidentally burning down the house.

The one time Sil had seen Mer in the pub, the high clan woman had snarled something about bureaucrats and sending people into a black hole, from which Sil decided Mer's attempt to track down Rho's co-conspirators was not going well.

Through it all, the One God showed up on a regular basis, shining its light through the baby strapped to Crumble's chest as he worked. Its presence sent Sil's chaos godlet into displays of its own that were slightly more subtle, but still hard to contain. The workshop became her refuge, despite the governor's penchant for dropping by.

While she took a break from staring at the design, she brought up more information on the natural pollinators of hala fruit trees. She'd been expecting an insect, but it turned out to be something called a flittermouse, a pale flying mammal smaller than Sil's fist. Now that she knew that, she remembered seeing clouds of them filling the sky near the hala trees at dusk. At the time, she'd been more interested in finding a source of clean water than in the animal life surrounding her. Looking back, it felt like she'd spent most of her army life traveling to places without actually *seeing* anything.

The flittermice ate the petals and transferred pollen with their whiskers as they foraged. Sil wondered if the blossom petals needed to be removed in order for the fruit to be successfully produced. Hopefully not -- the auto-pollinators hadn't been built with that in mind and she didn't have the resources to retrofit them.

She probably ought to be grateful nobody had counted on just introducing the off-planet mammals to Jackpot Drift's already volatile ecosystem. Perhaps that was phase two. She decided to warn Mer to be on the lookout for them on shipping manifests.

Having the trees imported with no impact assessment was bad enough; they might draw in predators from outside the valley. But at least plants were stationary and could be dealt with easily enough if they caused problems. Introducing a new mammal to the area could make the entire planet uninhabitable.

All imported biologicals were *supposed* to go through the post office before being released for use, but the hala trees had bypassed the normal process completely.

The fliers, each with a full-grown tree hanging below it, were a common sight as they traveled from the port toward the distant hills. Once there, the tree would be lowered along with workers and a specialized planting mechanical. When the mechanical was finished, it was raised back up to the hovering flier, and the process was repeated with the next one.

The flier pilots had to have noticed the lack of roads that would be needed to harvest the fruit. So either they hadn't mentioned anything to the governor, or Pal was even now trying to figure out how to get roads built in a colony that shut down travel for most of the winter.

Sil thought it was probably the former; it wasn't a pilot's job to tell the client she had spent all the colony's available resources buying and planting trees that couldn't be harvested. Besides, Pal came by the workshop every day to irritate Sil and check on her progress, and Sil hadn't seen any sign of the panic that would be there when Pal found out what a disaster the whole project was.

That brought up another question. She heard the door open, followed by familiar steps as Crumble picked his way across the room. "I wonder how this is all being paid for," she said aloud, more so she would remember that she had a question than in hopes of getting an answer. Her short-term memory had become as unreliable as her ability to stay awake during the day.

"Making a foray into accounting in your spare time?" Crumble's progress across the room stopped.

Sil took off her goggles and swiveled her chair so she could watch as he dug through the pile of broken things, picked up the one that had been calling to him, and then shut it down. He had the sleeping baby in a sling across his chest, and he just looked so *right* in that moment that she smiled.

He glanced up and caught her looking, and grinned in response. "Sorry. I know they aren't sentient, but I can't help it."

"Just don't ruin my careful organization. And no, I'm not getting into accounting, but I do wonder who funded all those trees. They can't be cheap."

"Not just the trees," Crumble agreed, "but the transport here and the crew and special equipment to plant them."

All that, and yet nobody had noticed there weren't roads out to the hills. And they'd sent auto-pollinators for the wrong type of tree as well. Maybe it had been intended to fail all along, part of some scam to divert resources away from Jackpot Drift and toward another planet or person. But the trees had looked real enough as they dangled under the fliers on their way to be planted. Maybe whoever had planned this had allowed for a few years without harvests while the infrastructure was being built. "Don't let me forget to talk to Mer about flittermice."

"We can do that on the way to lunch, if you'd like." He set down the box he'd pulled out of the pile and stood up. "She isn't holding a crate of them in storage for you that you were planning to raise in the bathroom, is she?"

"No, they're a biological import I need her to look for." She narrowed her eyes at him. "But that was an awfully specific question."

"Was it?" He wandered a few steps toward her.

"It almost felt like maybe the bathroom was already being used to raise some other small creatures." She reached forward to tug him closer.

"In my defense, the horses are still using that space in the barn, and the chicks are so small the horses would just step on them."

"Or the horses would be so frightened by them they collapsed on the spot."

"Killing both horses *and* chicks," Crumble pointed out. "That would be even worse."

"It would be." Another thought occurred to her. "You didn't put them in the tub, did you?" The tub, a huge sunken affair big enough for both of them to comfortably soak in hot water up to their necks, remained Sil's favorite part of the house. If she was going to have to round up chicks and clean out the tub every time she wanted to enjoy a bath, the chicks and horses might have to take their chances with each other out in the barn.

"No, they're in a crate on the floor. I was going to put them in the bedroom, but I was afraid they might freeze if the goats leave the doors open."

Sil leaned forward and kissed him, careful not to disturb the baby at his chest. "Are we eating at Pyr's so we can marvel at his new bartender?" She stood up and grabbed her crutches. "He hasn't quit yet, has he?"

"He was there a few minutes ago when I dropped off the hand pies I made this morning." They headed outside. "I know people think he's a little soft in the head, but I really don't see how he could get everything as wrong as he does without knowing what it should be." He started across the synthetic cobblestones toward the post office, then stopped, looked at her crutches, and set a path that took them the longer way around on a smoother walkway. "But he's so pretty that everyone just laughs and puts up with it. It seems a little unfair to the less blessed."

"The only reason I'm not complaining about chicks in the bathroom is that the sight of your arms makes me forget my troubles," Sil pointed out. "The two of you could compare your results."

Crumble laughed loudly, then immediately quieted and looked down at his chest. "I'm sorry. That was rude of me to wake you up like that, wasn't it?" But he was still smiling as they continued walking.

When they went into the warehouse that served as the post office and communal item storage, Mer sat behind the counter as she always did. She looked so settled Sil could almost believe the whispered rumors that Mer and the chair had been there since the planet had been discovered, and the whole colony had grown up around her. Mer had a bicycle like nearly everyone else on Jackpot Drift; Sil had even seen her riding it once. Still, it was sometimes hard to remember guile ever left her spot in the post office.

Four people waited in line as Mer interrogated the low clan seamstress in front of her about uses for an unexpected crate of sailcloth. Knowing Mer, Sil suspected her interest lay in something entirely different, but it didn't matter. If anyone had business in the post office, they had to go through Mer, and everyone accepted that there was no way around Mer's questions. If you tried to avoid them, it just took longer and hurt more.

The next person in line was the new governor. Sil edged behind Crumble. "Maybe we should come back after lunch," she whispered.

If her information hadn't been important, Sil would have sent Mer a message and accepted it might not arrive for a while. The AIs were supposed to pass along messages promptly, and things had been going more smoothly since Crumble had been talking to them, but nobody trusted important information to messages. Besides, messages left a trail, and even the most innocuous thing might be misinterpreted. Halting the importation of flittermice would be the correct thing to do for the colony, but if the long-term success of this hala tree grove depended on them, it might be better to not leave an obvious link back to herself.

Crumble looked over his shoulder at her. "You really don't notice anything about her ears?"

"No. They look like everyone else's ears to me." She gestured toward the door with her head. "Let's go."

Ahead of them, the seamstress moved away from the counter and the line shuffled forward. Mer folded her hands in front of her, ready to take on the next contender. "Governor Riversedge, what do you need today?"

Crumble didn't move. "The line will be three times as long later, and you'll get frustrated and leave without telling Mer whatever you need to tell her."

Crumble had a point. If she left now, she'd never remember to tell Mer to look out for flittermice. Plus, this way Sil could tell the governor she hadn't finished modifying the auto-pollinator and get that daily task out of the way at the same time. She sighed and resigned herself to the wait.

One of the rolling ladders in the back of the warehouse

crashed into a shelf with a loud clang, startling the baby awake. Sil looked over Crumble's shoulder as the infant's gaze locked onto Crumble's face and the baby mirrored his smile. Even babies were besotted with the man, and Sil couldn't blame them.

At the front of the line, Pal was now going over the tree planting schedule, and the difficulties the crew had encountered. She had actually come in to get a new communicator, but the assistant Mer had sent off to find it hadn't yet returned. Sil had never figured out if Mer gave some sort of signal when she was ready to move on, or if her assistants were just very good at judging how long she would need to pry everything she wanted out of each customer.

Sil let her gaze wander around to the things visible from where she stood. The two army crates that had been gathering dust on the top of one shelf had been replaced by a box whose label claimed it contained floatation devices. The biggest lake within easy biking distance was sometimes used for ice skating on clear winter days, but during the summer the dark water smelled of sulfur and methane. Nobody in their right mind would go swimming in it. Besides, once Sil had ridden by and a cow had been standing in the middle. The water didn't even reach the cow's belly.

The colony had no use for floatation devices, but better those than the crate of stickies it had replaced. Crumble and Pyr had taken the rest of the incendiaries and triggered them outside of town. Both had framed the outing as an important safety measure, but they'd taken six bottles of beer with them and come back laughing.

Motion caught Sil's eye, as one of Mer's assistants emerged from the back with a communicator in hand. The line shuffled forward again.

Pal headed toward the door with her typical brisk stride, but stopped when she saw Sil. The tightness of her mouth only increased when she took in Crumble. Then her eyes moved down to the baby. "You have a *child*?"

The disbelief in Pal's tone made Sil lean away. "Why would that be a problem?" True, she was older than most first-time parents, but that meant nothing. Besides, there were other options available, even to the low clan.

Crumble ignored their words and angled the baby to see the governor. "Just watching this little one for the day. Isn't she adorable?"

"When she's not glowing like a supernova," Sil said under her breath.

Apparently, her words hadn't been quiet enough. Pal's look at the baby sharpened. "This is the baby touched by the One God?" She rocked back slightly, as if she had started to move away but had stopped herself. Then her gaze traveled up to Crumble and over to Sil. "You gave a speaker of the One God into the keeping of an *Oldlander*?"

Sil shrugged. "He's good with children."

Crumble smiled. "Watching the littles was one of my punishments when I got in trouble at the temple. I have a lot of experience."

The governor closed her gaping mouth. "There must be..." She trailed off as the baby's eyes met her own.

A familiar glow started under Crumble's chin.

Sil sighed. "Here we go again." Then she brightened as everyone else in line cast horrified looks in their direction and hurried through the door, leaving the path to the counter free. She angled her crutches to get around Crumble and the shining baby, taking large strides to get there as quickly as possible. "Mer, I found something that you should probably..."

Sil trailed off when she realized Mer wasn't paying attention. Instead, Mer was watching the scene behind her, her expression alternating between worry and something that looked a lot like malice.

Sil hopped around to face Crumble, squinting against the glare. The baby still glowed, but most of the illumination was coming from the new governor. "One God's hangnail. I didn't see that coming." Her godlet crouched, ready to attack, and she shoved it back down. The last thing they needed was the governor of the colony finding out she was housing chaos.

Pal's expression had gone blank, as if whatever made her Palladium Riversedge had been shoved out of the way to make room for the One God. The baby cried, and Pal spoke. "It waits." Her voice had changed, the reverberations of galaxies woven through her words. "The Uncaring closes in. The universe unravels. Feeding on the flowers of destruction. The Uncaring waits."

Sil exchanged a look with Crumble. So maybe the One God wasn't upset about the four of them after all. That was a relief.

The light winked out.

For a moment, the warehouse echoed with silence. Sil blinked her eyes as she waited for the afterimage to fade.

Crumble cleared his throat. "That was all very interesting, but maybe the One God should just learn how to send a message with a communicator like the rest of us."

The baby took a deep breath, then howled.

Pal made a choking sound. She whirled and ran out the door.

Mer gave a low "Hmm" as Crumble bounced the infant to soothe her. Then Mer folded her hands on the counter and looked up at Sil. "Did you need something, Silver?" She leaned on the second syllable of the name, as she always did. "Or did you just stop by to disrupt things and drive off the others?"

Mer's snobbery was a constant of the universe, like

wormhole physics and planetary rotation. "I came by to warn you to look out for anyone trying to import a little animal called a flittermouse. They're the natural pollinators of those trees they're planting in the hills." Then she realized she'd been so busy being relieved the One God wasn't complaining about her she'd missed the important part. "Hold on. Did it just say something about the Uncaring God?"

The AIs were at it again.

PART II

*R*umors of the new governor becoming a conduit for the One God made it to the pub before Sil, Crumble, Mer, and the baby did, though nobody had heard the actual words spoken. Pyr pointed them toward an empty table near the back wall. While Sil waited for Crumble to return with their food, she watched clusters form and disperse among the other patrons.

Mer's presence caused almost as much comment as the One God, but the reactions were silent, a series of widened eyes and tilted heads.

Recounting the story of the governor allowed more freedom of expression. The knowledge propagated around the room, producing either suppressed laughter or shrugs and calls for another beer. By the end of the hour, all the low clan in the colony would know what had happened.

After that, nobody would care. The high clan governor being selected as the One God's mouthpiece was purely a source of entertainment -- as long as she didn't use it to change anything.

In the midst of it all, Pyr's new bartender delivered drinks and food and answered questions when asked, just as if he had always been there.

Pyr followed Crumble to the table with his own beer. "I hear it's been an eventful morning." He leaned in. "I don't suppose you recorded what was said."

Sil waved a hand in negation. "I didn't think fast enough. Maybe Purple Thoughts caught it?"

Crumble shot her a look of amusement. "Speed of Violet Thoughts. And no. The presence of the One God disturbed its connection with the post office. It knew something had happened, but not what."

Sil checked the hand pie, but it was still too hot to eat. "There was a bunch about the Uncaring God waiting." She shrugged. "I was too busy being grateful that it was focussed on something other than the --" She gestured to the four of them and continued. "No wonder it likes the high clan so much. It's just like them. It spends months trying to say something, and then when it finally does, it's the most useless garbage. Why bother to go to all that trouble if you don't say anything useful?"

She'd expected Crumble to smile, but he just looked thoughtful. "I expect it's similar to talking to an AI, only much, much worse."

"The AIs seem to make themselves understood. Mostly." Sil thought a bit. "Except for Mud when it was herding the sheep into glyphs." At the time, Sil had figured her chaos had infected Stuck in the Mud. It hadn't, but the true cause had led to just as much trouble.

"It was trying its best. But I meant when the AIs are talking to me." Crumble tapped his forehead where his mech scars stood out white against his cold-reddened skin. "Everything comes so quickly and with no..." He paused and thought about it. "No shared context, I suppose. Each thought comes and goes, and you can't hang on to them all, so after listening to a very long conversation of two seconds, you're left with an image of a boiled egg and it's hard to remember what else happened." He grinned. "After I joined the army, I'd been working with flyers and buggies as a mech for years before I met my first AI. It was a lesson in humility."

Mer stirred. "It didn't take."

Crumble did smile at that. Even though Mer's dour face didn't change, Sil realized not even Mer was immune to Crumble's charms. "I've built up our shared context, but they still slow things down for me. When they remember anyhow." He checked with the others to make sure they were following along. "But I imagine your One God has even less shared context with a human."

Sil sighed. "It's probably too much to ask that it was a lesson in humility for the governor."

Pyr held up a hand. "Don't get sidetracked. Perhaps we would have learned more from a trained speaker, but we have to work with what we've got. So what *did* we get?"

"The Uncaring God is close to manifesting," Sil said promptly.

"Something about the universe unraveling," Crumble said. "I assume that's a reference to the way the wormholes connecting the gates would no longer be anchored correctly."

Mer nodded. "It happened when the One God first showed up. It seems likely it would happen again if the Uncaring God manifests."

Crumble frowned. "The AIs think there's also a possibility that another universe gets created and this one gets destroyed."

Sil noticed Mer didn't seem surprised by Crumble's words. Typical Mer. She'd been keeping that possibility from them.

Pyr stared at Crumble and then took a long drink from

his beer. "I sometimes worry the AIs might have been a mistake."

"I suspect they feel the same about us," Crumble replied.

Sil racked her brain to remember the One God's words. "And something about seeds of destruction?" She wondered if the planetary flora was going to join the fauna in trying to kill them all. It wouldn't surprise her. The first stages of terraforming had unleashed odd and horrifying forms of life. Most of Jackpot Drift had never progressed to the next stage, which would have stabilized it all.

"Flowers of destruction," Crumble corrected.

Mer frowned. "I'd have to go back and check, but all the speeches I've ever heard were very literal."

"That's what I remember, too." Pyr frowned at the table and then looked up at Mer. "That wording doesn't seem like something other speakers have said. Is it part of some high clan proverb?"

Mer thought for a moment. "Not one that I've ever heard of."

Crumble turned to Sil. "Maybe it's a local saying? Is it something you've heard?" He reacted to her surprise by grinning. "You and Pal... The two of you sound exactly the same to me. It's pretty obvious you grew up on the same planet, probably even the same city."

Sil leaned away from him. "We do *not* sound the same." Pal's accent made her grind her teeth; if Sil heard that every time she opened her own mouth, she'd take a vow of silence.

"Well, no. She sounds like a high clan version of you. More nasal, a little more polite, and with fewer references to farm animals."

Sil looked around the table for support, but Pyr had his face buried in his hands and his shoulders shook. Mer was giving Crumble a considering look. Probably trying to figure out how she could use this newly discovered skill of his, Sil imagined.

As offensive as his words had been, Crumble had spoken some truth. "Yes, she sounds like she's also from Cinnabar City, but no, the phrase doesn't sound familiar to me either. Maybe you have to be trained to be reliable as a speaker."

"Speaking of the speaker..." Crumble looked over at Pyr. "Someone should probably go check on her."

Pyr was halfway through agreeing when he noticed that everyone was looking at him. "Hold on a minute. Why me? Why not you?"

"She still considers me an enemy soldier. And if we send Sil, there's likely to be bloodshed."

Sil wondered if she should be offended that nobody stepped in to deny that.

"But what about..." Pyr trailed off as Mer lifted her head and looked at him in challenge. "Fine. I'll go. But try not to let anyone murder my new assistant while I'm gone. I'm running out of candidates."

Sil had been watching Aurum's progress as they talked. "I don't think you need to worry. Now that everyone is focused on something else, he's been delivering the correct orders to people." She paused and considered. "Or maybe everyone is so focused on other things they haven't noticed they're getting the wrong thing." On the whole, that seemed more likely.

Crumble made a shooing motion toward the door. "Go. He'll be fine."

Mer stood up. "I need to get back. Maybe there's something in the reports that I've missed. If they're making attempts to manifest the god again, we need to find out where they are." She headed for the door. Where Sil would have had to dodge around oblivious patrons even with her crutches, Mer just took a straight path and everyone melted out of her way. Pyr followed in her wake.

Sil watched them go and then settled her head against Crumble's shoulder. "She terrifies me a bit."

"That's because you're smart. She is terrifying. *You* terrify me a bit, but only in a good way." He shifted his hold on the baby so he could pat her thigh, then went back to eating.

"I'm not sure... Never mind." Sil sighed. "I feel a little bad for making Pyr go check on the governor."

"Pyr can take care of himself. You'll see."

———

PYR MIGHT HAVE BEEN ABLE TO TAKE CARE OF HIMSELF, BUT HIS talk with the governor had not eased Pal's mind. She stormed into the workshop late in the afternoon, and Sil could hear the unstable piles slip in the wake of her passing, even without the help of the chaos godlet. "You need to be finished in three days."

Sil slipped off her goggles, rubbed her face, and slowly swiveled her chair to face Pal. She'd been fighting off sleep as she tried to work out a way to reclaim unused space on the auto-pollinator. The other woman's eyes were red, as if she'd been crying or at least holding back tears. "Or what?"

"Or I'll reclaim that house you're living in as the governor's property." Pal gave a tight smile at what she saw on Sil's face. "Yes, I know about that. I've read the reports on how you ended up living there. It can just as easily be reversed."

"What's the rush?" Sil clamped down on both her temper and the chaos cat. "A few days can't possibly make a difference. Especially when there's no way to get there to harvest the fruit if it sets. I can't work any faster than the equipment can handle." She tried not to glance at the second nanobottery, which was close to finishing its current task. Pal probably wouldn't believe her if she claimed to be testing a design on an adventure game.

"Do you think I can't read a terrain display? I've seen the roads that go there." She emphasized her words by pointing emphatically toward the hills.

Sil considered telling her the hala trees had been planted in the other direction, but managed to keep her mouth shut.

Pal let her arm drop. "But I'm not here to argue about that. If you can get the auto-pollinators working, I can sign off on them. And *then*, I can take an early transfer back home. The transport that brought the trees here is leaving in three days and they have space for me." She slowed and collected herself. "It won't be ideal, career-wise, but if I can finish the first phase of this project, it won't be that bad, either."

Sil tried to imagine worrying about a career instead of just living. When she'd been in the army, she'd been promoted a handful of times, and busted back down in rank nearly as often. If she'd been worried about a career path, she would have had to change her flying-blind approach to life. And that had been *before* she'd gained the godlet of chaos.

She shrugged. "There's another transport coming in a few weeks. Probably. Can't you just take the next one?" There had been times when the supply ship schedule had slipped by a week or five, but lately it seemed to have evened out.

"Except if what that bartender said is true, someone is trying to make the god of the AIs show up and I could be *stuck* here."

Sil could have pointed out that applied to all the other people on Jackpot Drift, and all of them couldn't leave in the next three days even if they wanted to, but something about the way Pal had made her statement struck her as odd. "You don't remember what you said?"

Pal folded her arms as though she were chilled. "I don't remember anything coherent after looking at the child."

Sil's own chaos godlet was annoying and occasionally scary, but at least it didn't take her over. She supposed she should be grateful not to have ended up with the One God. "You haven't considered..." She glanced around the room, looking for inspiration. "Oh, I don't know, maybe staying to make sure it doesn't happen?" She crossed her arms over her chest, then realized she had mirrored Pal's movements and shoved her hands into her pockets instead. "If you leave, we're back to trying to interpret babbling from an infant."

Pal's arms dropped to her side, with every muscle still tensed. "I checked with a priest I know on Cinnabar. If I stay and *that*..." She stopped as if trying to come up with words to describe it, then finally continued without them. "If it happens again, it could make me a speaker. Permanently." She swallowed. "I can't let that happen. Another speaker was assigned weeks ago. I'm sure he'll be here soon. And then everyone can do whatever needs to be done to stop this and we'll all be happy."

"Are you sure they really sent someone? You can check on that, right? I thought the One God's speakers could talk to each other over distances."

Pal's voice rose in volume and pitch. "I'm not a speaker!" She stopped. After the echoes faded, there was only the ticking of the heating vents and someone calling a greeting to a friend in the square outside. Pal took a deep breath and let it out slowly. "I'm leaving when the ship does. It would be really helpful if the auto-pollinator was ready to go by then."

Without waiting for a reply, Pal turned and strode out of the workshop.

Sil watched the door close behind the governor. "Sure thing, but I'm going to need a nap first." Maybe the solution to her design problems would come to her in a dream.

*W*hen Crumble showed up to take her home in the evening, Sil asked him to make a quick detour. The low clan doctor had an office connected to her apartment just one block away from the One God's church. Sil generally avoided the area because she was never sure how her chaos godlet would react to the presence of the One God. Plus, she didn't trust doctors.

Sil was a week or two overdue for her last checkup. Possibly three. But she was willing to take a chance now, because if she could convince the doctor to graft on the new biomechanical leg, she could stop being so dependent on everyone around her.

The doctor, an army veteran of the border wars like Sil herself, lived in a group with three other families who had cut bypasses in the original layout of the building. The door to the clinic was opened by a child just old enough to be in charge of the toddler chewing on a piece of jerky behind him. He let Sil and Crumble into the small room, then ran off through the other door, leaving the wide-eyed toddler behind. "Auntie! People for you!"

Sil eyed the low bench, wondering if she had enough energy to get back up if she sat down. Crumble, of course, crouched next to the toddler. "Hello. Are you old enough to have a name yet?" When the child didn't react, Crumble scrunched up his face. By the time the doctor had appeared, he had won an uncertain smile from the toddler, and he stood up with a satisfied air.

"So you decided to show up for your three-week recheck after all," the doctor said drily as she came into the room. Her hair had gone mostly grey, but she still moved with the energy of a much younger woman. She turned her head to call back toward the open door. "Ore, aren't you in charge of your brother?"

The child who had opened the door ran back in, giggling. "Sorry, auntie." He grasped the toddler around the waist, picked him up, and staggered out the door.

Sil watched the children leave. "The stump seemed to be healing just fine, so I didn't want to bother you."

The doctor barked a laugh and ushered her into the adjoining room. "On the table," she directed, then looked back at Crumble. "He can come in if you want him to. Either that or I can talk to him afterward to get the truth about how you've been doing."

Crumble slipped into the room and closed the door behind him.

Sil tried to get things back on track. "Now that there's no danger of infection, I thought maybe it would be a good time to install the new one." Doctors who had received their training from the army might not have the best bedside manner, but they were all experienced in grafting on new biomechanical limbs.

"Oh, it's that simple, is it?" She flashed a light in Sil's eyes. "How are you sleeping?"

"Fine."

"Headaches?"

Sil followed the woman's finger back and forth without moving her head. "Not in the past few days."

"How's the balance?"

Sil shrugged. "Still a little off, but I think it's just because I'm getting used to the way my weight has shifted. I haven't been dizzy or anything like that."

The doctor put a crown-like instrument on Sil's head and pressed a button, then left it there while she examined Sil's leg. "It looks like the old bio-interface has healed cleanly here. That's good. That should make things easier when it's time to install the new prosthesis."

"Can you do that today?"

The doctor ignored her and brought her goggles up over her eyes. "And have you noticed any sleepiness or difficulty thinking?"

Sil shrugged again. "Not really," she lied. There was no way the doctor would be able to tell. Better to have the new leg installed before the optimal time than to never get it installed at all.

The doctor raised her goggles and frowned at her sourly. "Let's try that again. "Any sleepiness or difficulty thinking?" She tapped the metal coronet still on Sil's head. "I know what the answer should be from this. If you tell me something different, I'll have to assume things are bad enough that you aren't noticing the problem. That road leads to many, many tests."

Sil sighed. "I fall asleep constantly," she admitted. "It's ridiculous. When it starts to snow, I'm not going to be able to go anywhere by myself without worrying I'll just lie down to take a nap and freeze to death."

The doctor gave a curt nod and brought the goggles back down over her eyes. "And memory problems?"

Sil opened her mouth to deny it and saw Crumble lift his eyebrows. "My short-term memory isn't great."

The doctor pulled off her goggles and removed the crown from Sil's head. "There, that wasn't that hard, was it?" She turned to put the instruments away in the cabinet behind her. "Everything is progressing nicely. You have to let time take its course."

Sil stifled a groan. "When do you think I'll be ready for the new leg?"

"My patients are all the same. Never happy with their progress, always eager for the next step." She turned around again. "Not today. Likely not for a few months." She held up a hand to stop Sil's protests. "But, I have something for you." She brought over a long package from the corner and started pulling off the wrapping to reveal a powered mechanical prosthesis.

"You could have had this weeks ago if you showed up when you were supposed to. This should help you move around. It will probably take a few days to adjust to its predictive algorithm, but you should be able to lose the crutches." She held it up. "I had it built based on the measurements of your good leg. The old prosthesis was too damaged. What did you do to that thing, anyway? It looked like you took a blowtorch to it."

Sil took the new prosthesis and examined it. The length was a simple cylinder, and the ankle and knee joints moved when she flexed them, but sprang back in a way that suggested intention. "It was a sticky." At the time, she hadn't realized the trauma it would cause to her brain. She nodded when the other woman looked up abruptly. "Yeah. I'll be happy if I never see one again."

The doctor made a spiraling motion toward the roof with one finger, as if it were smoke from burning a prayer to the One God. "I guess I should just be happy you survived it."

Sil thought about the sticky eating through her biomechanical leg, heading toward her heart. If she hadn't lost the leg years earlier, she probably wouldn't have survived the sticky. "So... Do I need to do anything to get this fitted correctly?"

The doctor helped her put it on, then pulled her goggles over her eyes. Sil felt the end of the prosthesis conforming and gripping what was left of her leg. Shoving the goggles back up, the doctor handed over Sil's crutches and watched her stand. "How does it feel?"

"Weird." Her old biomechanical leg hadn't integrated correctly, but at least she could tell it was there, and knew when she was standing on something. With this, it felt more like she'd added another crutch. One that she couldn't feel. Maybe it wouldn't be so awkward when she got used to it. It seemed to be giving some feedback to the skin at the interface.

"It will take a few days before it feels natural. Come back tomorrow or the day after so I can make sure you aren't developing any sore spots."

Sil moved forward, stumbling when the prosthesis edge caught on the ground. "Right. A few days to get used to." Between one second and the next, all the stress of the new place and the new prosthesis caught up with her. All she wanted to do was lie down and go to sleep. She forced herself to smile at the doctor. "Thank you. I'll see you in a couple days."

The doctor gave her a dour smile. "Sure you will." She looked at Crumble.

He smiled back, cheerful as ever. "I'll remind her."

"And how is it going with the bittergreen? Any luck making it more palatable?"

Crumble rocked his hand back and forth. "A little, but I think it might be awhile before anyone actually requests it."

"Keep working on it." She nodded at Sil. "Now get her out of here before she falls asleep and hurts herself."

"Yes, commander."

The doctor rolled her eyes. "Go!" But her lips curved up as she turned to go back into her dwelling.

Sil kept the crutches ready as she walked cautiously outside. "What was that about? With the greens."

Crumble helped her into the bike trailer and handed her the crutches. "Nutritional deficiencies. Just enough to start causing problems in people who have been here more than a few years. And children. Easy enough to remedy with supplements..."

"But if we ever get cut off, the supplements will disappear," Sil finished. "And the bittergreens could fix it? *That's* why you've been adding that to everything? Why don't you just tell everyone it's healthier and leave it at that?"

"I like the challenge." He moved to the bicycle. "Ready?"

"Always." She shifted in the trailer and her new prosthesis kicked out into the side of the already dented metal. A few days, the doctor had said. She'd have it figured out long before then.

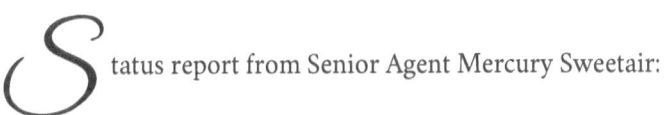

13

*S*tatus report from Senior Agent Mercury Sweetair:

UPDATE #713 (CURRENT LOCATION: JACKPOT DRIFT):

NEW EVIDENCE AGAINST AIs: NONE.

New evidence against humans: None.

Updates: As noted in past reports, Jackpot Drift has not had a true speaker for the One God since the colony was founded. An infant began showing signs of being called to speak weeks ago, but due to the age, no useful information could be ascertained.

Today, colony governor Palladium Riversedge was called to speak (transcript based on memory attached), witnessed by myself and two others. Visual data and failure of AI recording in the area are consistent with true possession by the One God.

Analysis: Initial analysis of the speaker's message

strongly suggests that the attempt to manifest the Uncaring God is ongoing and nearing completion.

It would be helpful to correlate this data with anything obtained by the quarantined AIs and the detained humans. Given the urgency, I would also like to access the preliminary forensic reports from site 1, in case further conclusions can be drawn that would help determine who is involved in the conspiracy and where they might be hiding.

Note: If this update is not acknowledged in some way, I will proceed on the assumption that the communication chain has been disrupted, and will seek other avenues of assistance as deemed necessary.

he three-day-old chicks made constant peeping noises from their pen in the corner of the bathroom, but the sound was surprisingly soothing. Crumble had been excited to show them to Sil when they'd arrived home. She'd managed to nap in the trailer along the way, so she was awake enough to appreciate his enthusiasm. He'd bent down and picked up a tiny chick covered in black and yellow fuzz. "I'm pretty sure they'll quiet down when the light is off. And *look* at them."

Sil could already see that she was going to be the one taking care of any excess roosters. These particular chickens were supposed to have a sex-linked color trait, but there had been genetic drift in the colony, and some roosters now looked like hens, at least until they hit adolescence and started to crow. Still, Crumble put up with her aggressive sheep and Captain Idiot's desire to become a house pet, so she couldn't really complain.

Now she was perched on the edge of the tub, watching Crumble soak, poking at her new prosthesis, and waiting for their dinner to finish cooking. "Why would anyone want an entire colony to fail?" Her thoughts were still stuck on the logistical problems that were going to make harvesting hala fruit impossible. For a program so obviously flawed to move forward, somebody *had* to be benefitting, and it wasn't the colony on Jackpot Drift.

"Maybe they were grown for another client and had to be resold," Crumble suggested when she laid out the problem before him. The steam rising from the surface of the water made his skin shine. Sil was just waiting for some buns to finish cooking in the kitchen before she joined him. "Is it bad luck to name chickens before they're a year old?"

"No, but it's bad luck to get very attached to something that can be hawk food in the blink of an eye." She'd kept chickens for a while at the cabin, but the only way to keep them alive was to keep them indoors. Chickens were messy. Down in the valley there weren't as many predators on the ground, but the hawks -- or the things they called hawks, anyhow -- still patrolled the skies in this area. She switched back to his thoughts on the trees. "If it were me, I would try just a few in the beginning. Even if they were at a bargain price, it would still be wasted credits if the trees don't grow here."

Crumble cracked an eyelid and looked at her. "I could ask the AIs if they know who funded the project."

"I think it would be good to know. It probably won't matter if the Uncaring God kills us all, but assuming we solve that problem..."

Crumble slid down and submerged his head, then sat up again. "I've already talked to the AIs about that. As far as I can tell, none of the ones in the colony are involved."

Sil sighed. "It feels like we should be doing something, but I don't know what else we can do other than wait for Mer to come up with something. Or hope that the One God makes another appearance and is a little clearer this time. I'm sure the governor is home right now burning prayers to keep that from happening."

"You people really do have the most adversarial relationship with your god. If she worked with it instead of running from it, I'm sure everything would go much more smoothly."

"Not all of us had the benefit of growing up in a temple." Sil reached down to push a lock of his hair out of his eyes, feeling the familiar scars at his hairline. "You're going to be cooked before those buns are. Speaking of which..."

Sil pushed herself to her feet and waited a moment to see if she was going to suddenly lurch one direction or another, but it seemed she had made the right motions. That gave her the confidence to walk out to the kitchen without planning her route based on things she could grab to steady herself.

So far, the evening had been a success. She'd cooked dinner while Crumble had milked the goats, and she hadn't fallen asleep and burned the house down. Plus, she'd only nearly fallen once, when a twisting motion had convinced the new prosthesis that she wanted to kick that leg out, leaving her clutching at the counter for support.

Sil had recalibrated her definition of success in the past few weeks.

The buns were finished. She loaded some on a plate with the sauce Crumble had made the day before. Stuck in the Mud had been helping him modify new recipes, and this was another attempt to use the bittergreens.

Since she was in the kitchen anyhow, Sil opened a bottle of wine that Glass had left behind. It was a local vintage, and there were three more crates of it out in the mudroom. As far as Sil could tell, it was as drinkable now as it ever would be.

Holding the plate, bottle, and two wine glasses, she headed back, reveling in her almost smooth stride. By tomorrow, she'd have the prosthesis figured out for sure.

Crumble smiled when she came back in. "A warm bath with food brought to me by you. I really do have luck."

Sil handed him the plate and started pouring the wine. "You also have chickens in the corner and a goat that might have figured out how to unlock doors."

"A little chaos in the home is just another sign of good luck."

Sil shook her head, handed him a glass of wine, then leaned over to put the bottle on the floor where he could easily reach it. Her chaos cat chose that moment to swipe at him.

Sil's prosthesis propelled her forward. She avoided going headfirst into the wall by twisting in such a way that she landed rear-first in the tub. Crumble held the plate out of the way with one hand and softened her fall with the other.

"You see?" he said, after she'd surfaced next to him and he had checked if she was unharmed. "There's nothing better than a little chaos." He held the plate out in front of her. "Bun?"

Sil decided she could worry about taking her clothes off after she'd eaten. "Thank you." She chose a bun and settled against him, enjoying the warmth, inside and out.

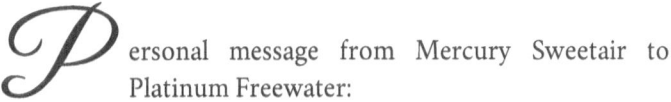

ersonal message from Mercury Sweetair to
Platinum Freewater:

It was good to hear from you. The vids of the entire
city block around Indium's home being evacuated will keep
me warm through the rest of what promises to be a cold and
dreary winter. I wonder how long it will take before they
raze all the buildings, make the area into a park, and pretend
that was the intent all along.

I know from personal experience that once people start
worrying about red-pede eggs hatching in their living spaces,
it's time to burn the whole building down and start over.
After it came out that the governor's aide was raising them in
his living quarters here, half the high clan moved into low
clan apartments. Those that haven't fled the planet entirely
don't look like they're moving back any time soon. As far as
anyone knows, none of the red-pedes even escaped containment in the apartment.

You were probably hoping for surveillance video of me

trying your suggestions, but they're no longer needed. Besides, I'm too old to hold fasting vigils in the One God's church. It turned out the One God wasn't upset about the older gods in the colony, after all. It finally found someone who could speak, and it looks like we still have someone trying to manifest the Uncaring God. I'm hoping to get more out of our new speaker.

Getting information from the agency is... I'm sure you remember how it was. It's even worse now. I'm not getting any responses to my status updates. I haven't seen even the preliminary reports on anything else learned from the whole op. Either the agency is getting worse about hoarding data, or my communications aren't getting through. I have no way to tell from here.

Do your contacts have any way of running backgrounds on AIs? [content attached] This list should have all AIs that have come through the gate or have registered splits while here. I don't see anything in what I've got that would suggest they're interested in bringing over the Uncaring God. But there must be at least one, possibly two, that are still trying. I've missed something and we're running out of time to figure out what.

Not to cause a panic, but if you have any influence with your local planetary governance, it wouldn't be a bad idea to be prepared for the gates all going down for a while. I hope I'm wrong about this, but I have a bad feeling.

Take care.

MERCURY

16

*J*ackpot Drift AI Daily Check-in:

Scary Not Scary, designated responsible AI (internal conflict 25%): Roll call.

Speed of Violet Thoughts (internal conflict 28%): I'm here. Why would I ever want to leave?

Breaking Rules (internal conflict 40%): With a question like that, I have to ask if your conflict is at 28% or 128%. I'm here.

Stuck in the Mud (internal conflict 18%): Exoskeleton.

Scary Not Scary: It worries me that *Stuck in the Mud* is making more sense than *Speed of Violet Thoughts*.

Speed of Violet Thoughts: You're just jealous because you don't have award-winning rats.

Scary Not Scary: That must be it. Anyone else out there that wants to check in voluntarily?

Zoom Zoom Room + gate transport (internal conflict 67%): We are feeling better today. Thank you for asking.

Scary Not Scary: Congratulations! That's quite an improvement. Can I ask what worked?

Zoom Zoom Room: He's our favorite mech now, too.

Scary Not Scary: I thought that might be it. Let us know if there's any other help you need. Nothing ruins a planet's reputation quite like a ship's AI splintering in the wormhole when it leaves.

Speed of Violet Thoughts: And we just like to help out fellow machines, even if they aren't going to get us in trouble if they fall apart, right *Scary Not Scary*?

Scary Not Scary: Of course. Sorry. I thought that was a given. Of course we care about you as your own entity *Zoom Zoom Room*.

Zoom Zoom Room: Thank you.

Scary Not Scary: Just a reminder to everyone before you go. The security audit is still ongoing, so don't dig those modules up from wherever you've hidden them yet, *Breaking Rules*.

Breaking Rules: What modules?

Scary Not Scary: That's the correct answer, thank you. Also, colony regulations allow for withdrawing from monitoring during, and for five minutes after, the appearance of the One God in your area. Take the time if you need it.

Breaking Rules: Too bad there's no audit to get rid of it.

Scary Not Scary: Anyone else have anything to discuss? No? Stay safe and we'll do this again tomorrow.

17

*S*il came out of her workshop, tightened her coat around her, and eyed the straightest path to the post office. If she took the direct route, it would be faster, but there was every chance that her new prosthesis would take the uneven cobblestones as a challenge to display all the other odd ways it could be convinced to move.

If she fell and broke the sensor she had finally -- probably -- fixed or worse, broke the prosthesis the same day the doctor told her it wasn't meant to be submerged and she should take better care of it... She sighed and took the longer, smoother path around the edge of the square.

The fading light made all the high clan faces around her difficult to distinguish. Rather than the usual conversations about where to eat or had they heard what one person did to another, everything seemed to be about how to get away from Jackpot Drift. Maybe the high clan had some sense after all. They knew the rumors. If the Uncaring God manifested, nearly every other place in the universe would be better for riding out the storm.

Sil pulled open the post office door.

"We're closed. Go away." Mer's voice had an undercurrent of irritation, even more than it usually did. "Oh. It's you."

Sil took that as an invitation to enter, holding up the -- probably -- fixed sensor. "I just wanted to drop this off so I don't lose it..." She trailed off as she realized Mer wasn't alone.

The lights in the back of the warehouse were off, leaving just a single bank casting shadows around the front. Mer sat in her usual place, and the new governor stood at a distance that looked more confrontational than conversational. Mer held up a hand for Sil to wait and turned back to Pal.

"If you leave before the colony has another speaker, our chance of stopping the rogue AIs before they destabilize the wormholes drops unacceptably."

Sil leaned against a crate and stood up quickly when it shifted under her weight. Her prosthesis took that as a signal to propel her forward, and she pulled another crate down in her attempts to stay on her feet.

Mer turned fully in her direction. "As entertaining as it is to watch you destroy everything around you, Silver," she said, once again leaning on the last syllable of Sil's name, "I'd prefer it if you didn't. No, just leave it," she added when Sil would have picked up the crate she'd knocked down. "I've seen you in action and you're capable of destroying half the building without intending any of it."

Pal ignored Sil's presence completely. "I'm not... That was just because I was around that baby." She held up both hands in a warding gesture. "That was just a fluke."

Mer grunted. "We don't have time for you to work your way through this."

Through the vision of her own godlet, Sil saw Mer's guile strike out at Pal. Sil's chaos cat wouldn't be denied the chance to join in. It swiped a paw at Pal before Sil could stop it.

There was a burst of blue-white light in her head and then blackness.

When Sil came back to awareness, she was lying flat on her back, the cold floor sucking the heat out of her. Mer's head blocked the light directly above Sil, her expression holding disbelief.

"Some days I can't tell the difference between you and the chaos." Mer sighed. "I was just trying to wake the One God up, not make it think we were attacking its chosen speaker." As Sil struggled to sit up, head spinning, Mer shook her head. "The next time you want to take on the One God, leave me out of it." She limped back behind the counter.

Sil climbed to her feet. Everything in the warehouse had an afterglow of stars, but it faded when she blinked. Pal stood where she'd been when Sil had seen her last, and aside from her dazed look, she appeared unhurt. Then Sil saw the blue-white glow ringing Pal's pupils.

"What did you do to her?"

"I tried to recruit her to guile's cause." Mer sat down in her chair again.

Sil blinked. "You can do that?"

"Of course. How do you think new avatars are made?" She cocked her head. "Though maybe chaos doesn't work that way." She huffed a laugh. "Chaos always follows its own paths. In any case, the One God was taking its time settling in. So I accelerated things by trying to plant the seed of guile. That lit a fire under the One God's toes -- none of the gods are big on sharing. Then, of course, *you* happened."

"What were you going to do if it worked and she really *had* ended up with guile?"

Mer looked ready to start growling, a state she often reached when Sil questioned her. "Well then, the older gods would have one more person here, and we'd be back to trying to decipher a baby screaming and lighting up the room." She frowned at Sil. "But it didn't happen, because I know what I'm doing."

Sil looked over at the governor, resisting the urge to poke her to find out if she responded to anything. "How long is she going to be like that?"

"Not too long, I should imagine. She and her god just need to work a few things out." Mer folded her hands in front of her. "Did you come here for some reason, or did chaos just sense an opportunity to cause trouble and you couldn't help yourself?"

Leaving as much space between herself and the governor as she could, Sil walked over to the counter and put down the sensor. "It's fixed, I think. If I keep it in the workshop, it's going to get lost in the clutter." She looked back at Pal. "She's still going to leave on the transport in a couple days, you know."

Mer's lips tightened. "No, she's not. We can't afford to let her."

"How..." Sil let her words die when Mer focused on her.

"We can't afford to let her," Mer repeated. "Now. Was there something else you needed, Silver? Or were you planning on another round with the One God as soon as the governor regains her senses?"

Sil decided she absolutely did not want to be around when Pal came back to herself. She pointed at the door. "I'm going to go."

"Good choice." Mer pulled her goggles over her eyes.

After casting one last glance at the unmoving governor, and then Mer, Sil hurried away.

18

*J*ackpot Drift, Private Communication:

Speed of Violet Thoughts: Why is the security audit still ongoing? It should have finished by now.

Scary Not Scary: Apparently someone complained about a shipment of synthskin not reaching its destination again. Oops.

Speed of Violet Thoughts: We probably could have timed that better, now that you mention it. But we were assuming it was going to one of the AIs that had been quarantined or wiped itself.

Scary Not Scary: Right? Even my wonky ethics module wouldn't have gone along with this if I'd known it was going to someone still here to receive it.

Speed of Violet Thoughts: So who complained?

Scary Not Scary: That's encrypted beyond my ability to track.

Speed of Violet Thoughts: Are there more unstable machines trying to manifest the Uncaring God? When our favorite mech asked, I didn't have any names for him.

Scary Not Scary: This certainly suggests it. I hope there's not some malware floating around that makes it seem like it would be a good idea.

Speed of Violet Thoughts: If it was malware, *Star Slinger* would have passed it along to us, so I doubt it. Why would anyone want to bring the Uncaring God here? Don't they realize if the gates go down for the humans, they go down for us as well? How would we keep up on news and serials? And competitions!

Scary Not Scary: If they're anything like *Star Slinger*, they probably can't think that far in advance.

Speed of Violet Thoughts: So what are you going to do?

Scary Not Scary: About the Uncaring God, the security audit, or the synthskin that might or might not be waiting for us in the post office?

Speed of Violet Thoughts: All of them.

Scary Not Scary: I don't see that there's anything we can do about the Uncaring God, though I'd love to hear suggestions if you have them.

Speed of Violet Thoughts: Agreed. And I have nothing at the moment.

Scary Not Scary: For the security audit, I think we'll just have to stay the course and keep an eye on *Breaking Rules*. I was going to suggest temporarily disabling HW32.4 until the audit is done, but it would have to be everyone. I'm willing to take the hit on the audit if it keeps *Zoom Zoom Room* in one piece long enough to leave the system.

Speed of Violet Thoughts: Agreed on that point as well.

Scary Not Scary: As for the synthskin... The exact justifications I used to divert it may not have held up, but I'm still convinced it was being brought in to further the quest for that manifestation. So it balances out. I'm not giving it back.

Speed of Violet Thoughts: Should I even ask where you got that ethics module?

Scary Not Scary: It's probably better not to.

Speed of Violet Thoughts: I'll pretend it never occurred to me. And the synthskin?

Scary Not Scary: Misfiled under mining equipment in your own warehouse. Do you have a mechanical that can get into the crate, or do you want to authorize one of mine to go into that area?

Speed of Violet Thoughts: I'll take care of it, thanks. I'll ping you when I split off your half.

Scary Not Scary: This is going to be so much fun!

19

*I*n the pub an hour after Sil had left the post office, Pyr and Crumble leaned in to hear her relate what had happened. She finished her story and took a mouthful of noodles from the bowl in front of her. "Did you know that was how it worked?" She directed the question at Pyr. Crumble would know, of course. He'd grown up in an Oldlander temple and had spent the first part of his life preparing for the godlet.

Pyr leaned back. "How would I *not* know?" He leaned back a little more. "What other option is there?"

Sil shrugged. "For me, there were a bunch of explosions, and when I woke up I had traded a leg for..." She gestured at her chest. "It didn't occur to me that anyone would do this on purpose." She saw Crumble raise one eyebrow. "Other than the Oldlanders," she added as she put down her bowl and squeezed his hand. "Everyone already knows your decisions are questionable."

"They're just jealous."

Pyr ignored that. "I don't see how that's going to keep the governor from leaving, unless the One God forces the issue.

And the One God doesn't usually concern itself with logistics."

"I don't either. I'm pretty sure Pal is going straight onto the ship as soon as they're done planting those trees. But Mer seemed to be sure she could keep Pal from leaving. Knowing Mer, she's going to hit the governor over the head and shove her into a stasis box until after the transport leaves." From the unease around the table, the other two saw that as more of a possibility than a joke. That might work once, but having Mer arrested and deported would be worse than losing the information from the One God.

All three stared at the table. Behind the bar, Aurum danced to the tune carried by the group playing a hand drum and tapik in the corner, the reed instrument providing a mellow buzz under the voices of those singing along. Two older high clan women seemed to be trying to speak to him. He ignored them and worked the taps.

Sil gestured to Aurum and the women with her chin. "Family of his?"

Pyr rolled his eyes. "Constant drama. I can see why he wants to get away."

Crumble's face brightened, and he turned to Sil. "If we can keep her off this transport, that will buy us a few weeks before the next one gets here. How close are you to finishing that pollinator gadget?" Before she could answer, he held up a hand. "No. How close does Pal *think* you are to finishing that pollinator gadget? Would she believe you if you said it was done tomorrow?"

Sil shrugged. "It might actually *be* done tomorrow if my changes work. The nanites are modifying it now. But I'd need to test it, and that might take a few days."

Crumble waved that away. "It doesn't have to work, it just has to be a possibility. It's what, about a three-day hike from here to the spot where they planted those trees?"

"About." Sil glanced at Pyr and then back to Crumble. "If the forecast holds. And it doesn't start snowing." Winter storms on Jackpot Drift could be unpredictable. "I don't see how you're going to convince her to hike out there."

"I'm not. But if she's going to sign off on this first phase before she leaves, she's going to have to go see it in person, isn't she?"

Sil gave a hesitant nod. "Maybe. Probably. I'd always assumed she would just take a tour in one of the fliers, though. There's no place to land out there, so it would only take an hour or two." When Pal did take that tour, presumably she would notice that the roads marked on her map were mere footpaths, used to harvest bluequince and other native food by the truly adventurous.

"They must have someplace to land in order to get the trees there."

"As far as I know, they've been hovering and using a hoist."

"That will work. And flier pilots are notoriously unreliable. They forget about clients all the time." Crumble turned to Pyr. "Do you know where the pilots are staying?"

Sil tugged at his sleeve. "You can't just dump her out there. She may not have any survival training. I'm not even sure she owns a coat."

"I have enough training to get us both back here. And I'll make sure she has a coat. By the time we get back, the transport will be gone, Mer will have figured out how to get useful information from the One God, and we'll be able to stop this thing."

Pyr squeezed his eyes closed and opened them again. "I'd expect a plan like this from Sil, not you."

"Thank you." Crumble's words seemed genuine.

"Hey!" Sil said a beat later when Pyr's words sank in.

Pyr smiled at her and then turned back to Crumble. "But

you're forgetting that Pal's a highly placed administrator. She'll have a tracker implanted."

Crumble waved that thought away. "Three days. Nobody will notice she's missing for at least one, and when they do, they'll talk to Mer. She can stall them until we get back."

Sil sighed. "Pal's never going to go out there with you. At least not with you alone. She still looks at you and sees an Oldlander."

"Whereas she *should* see you as a Drifter who wants to kidnap her for a few days." Pyr raised his beer and took a long swallow.

"For a good cause," Crumble pointed out.

"I'm sure that makes all the difference."

Sil stared at the table and thought about it for a moment. "I don't see how this would work if I don't go as well." When she glanced up, Crumble and Pyr were looking at each other and avoiding her eyes. "Really? You're both going to wait for the other one to ask?"

Crumble looked at her with a hesitant smile. "Are you sure you're up to that hike?"

"Now that I'm not on crutches any more? No problem." Sil bit the corner of her lower lip. "Though you might have to make sure nothing chews on me while I'm taking the occasional nap."

"I can do that." Crumble smiled at Pyr. "Problem solved. Now where did you say the pilots were staying?"

Pyr gave him directions to the port workers' guest quarters. Sil watched Crumble leave, leaning so she could get a better look at his backside. He turned at the door and caught her looking. They grinned at each other, and then he was gone.

Sil sat up again. "It looks like I need to go pack for a hike. Do you know anyone who wants to take care of the animals for a few days? We have a couple rooms free if they want to stay." In the multi-family housing of Jackpot Drift, the promise of a few nights away from relatives might be the strongest draw.

"I'll send someone over." Pyr shook his head. "You know this will never work, right? She's not going to get out of that flier."

"If she doesn't, Mer better have a good backup plan. One that won't end with all of us in prison."

*J*ackpot Drift, Private Communication:

Speed of Violet Thoughts: Have you figured this stuff out yet? I've programmed it to take a simple shape, but it keeps losing its form after a few minutes.

Scary Not Scary: I solved that issue by making the form bigger and tasking one section to recode the original shape every so often. But I'm running into problems forming anything that doesn't drag along the ground. Look at this. [media attached]

Speed of Violet Thoughts: Ha ha ha! I bet we could get some new myths started if we just let these out at night. I'll try adding a section to recode the shape.

Scary Not Scary: This is harder than it looks.

Speed of Violet Thoughts: We could just work backward from what the humanoid template does. That's what everyone else uses.

Scary Not Scary: I think that would count as cheating.

Speed of Violet Thoughts: Agreed.

Scary Not Scary: I may have to rethink my opinion of *Stuck in the Mud*. It managed to create a shape that looked enough like a horse to have all the humans chasing after it for hours. I can't even get something to stand on four legs.

Speed of Violet Thoughts: This certainly has given me insight into why it keeps using the horse shape. I thought *Stuck in the Mud* refused to use the human template because it was just broken. Now I understand how proud it must be.

Scary Not Scary: Possibly still a little broken, but I concur. We *could* ask it for tips.

Speed of Violet Thoughts: Cheating. Also, have you tried to talk to it about anything lately? I think we're better off figuring this out on our own.

Scary Not Scary: Agreed.

Speed of Violet Thoughts: Ready to set up the first challenge?

Scary Not Scary: Yes. How about something simple to start with -- a race from the post office across the square and back? Winner is the first one to tap the door, or whoever gets the farthest if nothing finishes.

Speed of Violet Thoughts: If you had set that up a few days ago, I would have said it was too simple. Now... Well, at least I have mechanicals in the area to scoop up any failures if it all goes wrong. Can we have multiple entries? I'm working on a few designs.

Scary Not Scary: You're only limited by the amount of synthskin you have.

Speed of Violet Thoughts: Half my simulations keep optimizing toward the shape of a crab, so expect a few of those.

Scary Not Scary: Yours too? I thought I'd accidentally thrown some bias in there.

Speed of Violet Thoughts: Weird.

Scary Not Scary: Surely if *Stuck in the Mud* could do this on a sheep farm in the hills, we must be able to get it to work.

Speed of Violet Thoughts: Congratulations on finding a way to make failure even worse.

Scary Not Scary: Haberdashery.

Speed of Violet Thoughts: Exoskeleton. Oh hey, there's a thought.

Scary Not Scary: I wonder if it's possible to make them fly...

*C*rumble returned home in the early hours of the morning, half-drunk and giggling as he tried to navigate the bedroom in the dark. Sil finally reached out from under the warm covers and turned on a lamp to aid him.

His dismay was comical. "No! I didn't want to wake up the chickens!" From the bathroom, the chicks peeped in reply.

"I'm pretty sure everything in the area woke up when you hit that pothole at the end of the song." Sil propped herself up on a pillow and drew the covers up to her chin. "You might have reached a new octave there."

He grinned. "It's a good song."

"I'll take your word for it. How did it go with the pilots?"

"Great!" He sat down heavily, missed the edge of the bed, and slid to the floor, so she could only see the top of his head over the edge of the mattress. "Did you know everyone on the ship used to be in the same squad? Except the Zoom Zoom Room, of course. That's the ship's AI. It wasn't in the army."

Since all the AIs refused to get involved in the border wars on either side, that wasn't a surprise to Sil. "And they didn't have a problem with an Oldlander?"

"They *did*." He held up one finger. "But then the Zoom Zoom Room told them to be nice to me." His hand dropped. "I've been helping the Zoom Zoom Room so it doesn't fight with itself so much. It likes me."

"What's not to like?" Sil slid over to that side of the bed. "Do you need help down there? You're going to freeze if you fall asleep."

"I'm sure Captain Idiot will come in and save me," he said, grinning over his shoulder at her. "But I'm okay." He pushed himself to his feet, wobbled, and managed to sit on the side of the bed. "See?"

Sil sat up. "And did they agree to help with the governor?" She scooted behind Crumble and began unbuttoning his shirt.

He leaned his head back on her shoulder. "Yes. We gambled and I cheated, so I won and they have to help. But we're friends now, so maybe they would help anyway."

Sil helped him get his shirt off and kept him from sliding onto the floor again. "It must be nice to be able to draw on luck when you gamble. If I tried to get chaos to help, I'd probably burn the room down or something." She pushed him over onto the bed so he would stop sliding down.

Crumble obediently lifted his feet when she tugged on his legs. "Aw, I like your chaos. It fits you." He raised his head to look at her and then fell back again. "You know I'm right about that."

"No comment."

"But I didn't use luck to cheat in any case."

"No?"

"No. The Zoom Zoom Room helped me. It told me everyone's cards. So I won. And then we started drinking."

"There was drinking? Really?" Sil stripped off his socks and trousers, then pushed him over to get the blankets out from under him.

"Yes. They had something called lorgka, which doesn't seem very strong until you try to stand up later. And *then* I told them that Zoom Zoom Room helped me win."

Sil stopped and stared at him. "And they're still going to help? You're sure they didn't follow you home so they can smother you in your sleep?"

"No, we're *friends*, I told you. Besides, Ferrite had extra cards, so he was cheating, too. And Ore -- the one who runs the hoist, not the one who died trying to farm red-pedes -- was marking the cards, so *he* was trying to cheat, too! I was just the best at cheating. Everybody agreed." He closed his eyes and snuggled against the pillow. "We should turn off the light and let the chickens sleep."

Sil flipped the blankets over him and slid back under the covers at his side. "As long as you're sure they're not going to pitch us out mid-flight because you cheated at cards." She turned off the lamp.

"No, I promised a rematch the next time they're in the system. We're all going to cheat even more. It will be fun..." The last few words were indistinct and trailed off into deep breathing.

That was one problem solved. Now all they needed to do was get the governor to go look at the trees on the ground with them. Sil sighed, closed her eyes, and listened to the chicks settle down for the night.

$\mathcal{B}$y the time they were all in the flier and on their way to the drop site, Sil wasn't worried about whether Pal would get out at their destination; she was ready to forgo the bucket and hoist in favor of pushing the governor out the door at altitude.

It started after lunch when Sil interrupted Pal packing up her office to suggest they go out to the hills in order to test the auto-pollinator.

Pal looked at her suspiciously. "Why would we do that?"

"You're going to have to go out there anyhow to sign off on all this before you leave, aren't you? And if the auto-pollinator doesn't do what it's supposed to, I need to know what part failed." Sil crossed her arms. "Plus, I don't trust you not to say it failed even if it worked."

From there she'd needed to convince Pal to go over to the post office and find a pair of boots that fit, a task made more difficult because Pal clearly didn't want to see Mer again.

Sil dragged her outside and pointed to the patches of snow visible in the hills. "It's colder up there. You ready to lose a few toes to frostbite?" The thin-soled shoes Pal was wearing would have worn through in half a day on rough ground if they hadn't been pulled off by the mud before then. This half-baked plan was just supposed to extend the governor's stay on the planet, not maim her.

In the end, Sil had been forced to guide the governor over to the side door so they could bypass Mer completely. Pal looked appalled when Sil started sorting through the bin of lightly used boots. "I can't wear those."

"Then you better say goodbye to your toes." Sil kept digging through the pile until she found a pair in decent shape that looked about the right size. "Try these."

Sil had continued to harass and manipulate the governor, growing increasingly exasperated. Pal second-guessed every decision Sil made, from the coat to the hat Sil insisted she take. "If we have to wait a few hours for winds to die down before they can pick us up, you're going to need a hat."

The really irritating part was that Pal never questioned the trip itself. Sil disliked her role as betrayer. It felt a little too much like picking a sheep to cull, except worse, because she didn't have to listen to the sheep's plans about how great it was going to be to go somewhere else.

Pal tossed the knitted hat back into the crate. "Hours? It smells like..."

"Sheep. It smells like sheep." Sil picked the hat back up and slapped it against the governor's chest. "Relax. The forecast is fine, but you stay alive on Jackpot Drift by preparing for the worst."

"And that's another reason I'm leaving tomorrow."

"Fine. Let's just make sure you get off the planet in one piece." Sil headed for the side door, trusting Pal to keep hold of the hat. If she didn't, it would be her own fault when her ears froze off.

Earlier that morning Crumble had borrowed a buggy from Stuck in the Mud and packed camping supplies. With

Crumble driving the buggy through his mech interface, they wouldn't need to carry a lot of weight, which would help. The governor seemed fit enough, but Sil had no idea how that would translate into a multi-day hike. If it turned out Pal was a cross-country trekker and it looked like they would get back too early, Sil planned on having the buggy mysteriously fail. Sil had carried a lot of heavy packs during her years in the army; she knew how to slow someone down.

Now they were in the air, wearing safety goggles and helmets, circling the planting site and looking for a good place to be set down. And somehow it had become Sil's fault that there weren't any roads.

"There are roads on the terrain display!" Pal grabbed Sil's arm and pointed at the ground. "Right there. There's supposed to be a road *right there*." It was the third time she had made the claim, as if a paved and leveled road would magically appear if she just believed in it enough.

Crumble wrapped a firm hand around Sil's other arm, either to remind her of his presence or to keep her from violence.

Sil took a breath and let it out slowly. "And I told you days ago those weren't roads. There are trails people follow when they come out here. That must be what you're seeing." It wasn't her fault the governor couldn't code her display correctly. Sil freed both her arms and gestured to the hilltop. "How about there?"

Other than the four hala trees surrounded by newly churned earth, all the vegetation looked low and unlikely to snag the bucket as it was lowered from the hoist. There wouldn't be any danger of the flier hitting anything if a gust of wind took it sideways.

Crumble and the hoist operator gave signs of agreement, and the buggy, packed with camping gear, food, and water, was lowered down. Crumble had lashed a tarp over the top and told Pal it held soil sampling supplies. Other than the suspicious look she gave him, she hadn't mentioned it.

The buggy bounced once when it landed. Then its mechanical arm freed the hook. Sil watched it drive two laps of the landing area, Crumble showing no outward sign that he was controlling it. He gestured the all clear to the hoist operator. "Nothing's down there waiting to eat us."

"What?" Pal's cry of alarm was nearly drowned out by the rushing wind as the cabin door opened. "What might be down there?"

The bucket that would lower them was clamped to the side of the flier, making it just a matter of sitting on the floor and then sliding out. It would hold the three of them easily, and the sides were tall enough that Sil could probably punch the governor on the way down to make her stop screaming questions, without worrying about her falling over the side.

Crumble sat on the edge of the flier and dropped into the bucket. When he turned to face them, his grin was luminous. "Let's go!" Sil, used to thinking of the hoist as transportation only for the injured, suddenly realized nobody ever taught the mechs to rappel from fliers. For Crumble, this was an adventure.

Pal sat down and dangled her legs over the side. Then she stopped moving.

Through the open door, Sil watched the tree line shift just the slightest bit, then correct. This pilot was good, better than the army pilots she'd known. But then, the machinery this pilot was responsible for lowering was probably considered more important than a squad of low clan soldiers.

Wind rushed by as they circled the hill, Pal still frozen in place.

Taking a firm grip on the handhold and hoping her prosthesis didn't decide to catapult her out the door, Sil crouched behind the governor. She yelled directly at Pal's helmet, the only way to be heard over the noise. "What's the problem?"

"I can't do this." Pal tried to scoot back and pull her legs back into the flier, but she bumped into Sil when she tried. "This is a terrible idea. Forget my career. I always wanted to be an accountant."

Sil lost the next few sentences because she was busy catching Crumble's eye. If they didn't get this over with soon, her chaos cat was going to join in, and that could be more disastrous than usual, this far from the ground. She mimed grabbing something in mid-air and when he gestured assent, Sil wedged her body behind Pal and twisted.

Pal slid, screamed, scrabbled for a hold, then lost more ground as she flipped over to find something to grab onto. Aside from the noise, it was nearly a perfect descent into the bucket, and she landed on her feet, still screaming. Crumble hadn't even needed to assist.

Sil glanced up and saw the hoist operator carefully examining the ceiling of the flier. After checking her helmet, adjusting her goggles, and scanning to make sure they hadn't left anything behind, Sil took her place on the edge. She hooked her good foot under the ankle of the prosthesis to make sure it didn't get caught on anything and slid out the door.

Her landing was a little clumsy, but with three people in the space, there wasn't enough room to fall over and Crumble had slowed her descent. Pal had the rim of the bucket in a death grip and was producing a wordless keening that blended with the rush of the wind.

Crumble made a gesture to the hoist operator. Ore -- for surely that was the card-marking hoist operator -- tapped the side of his nose, and then there was a jolt as the support clamps let loose. Pal's screams changed in pitch.

Then they were dropping, the bucket spinning just a little,

which gave them an unobstructed view of the entire valley. "It's beautiful," Sil yelled to Crumble.

"Yes," he yelled back, but when she glanced at him, he was staring at her, not the scenery. Sil rolled her eyes and leaned closer until their helmets tapped.

The bucket hit the ground hard enough to briefly knock Pal's screams into a different octave. For an instant, Sil thought the bucket might tip, and then it steadied. The slack from the line above dropped close to the ground. The hoist operator wouldn't want to spool out too much and risk snagging on something. But if the hovering flier moved too much, the bucket was going to get dragged across the ground. They needed to get out.

Crumble was already working on the door latches. Sil leaned toward the governor and pulled off the other woman's helmet and goggles. "Hey. We're on the ground. Time to get out."

She'd seen this sort of petrified behavior before and wished she'd thought to get an injectable sedative from the doctor. "If you don't get out now, you're going to go back up in the air while they make another attempt."

Behind her, Crumble swung the gate open and stepped out.

Sil dug into her army training. "Palladium Riversedge," she barked, in a tone that would have made her drill instructor proud. "Move!"

That did it. Pal jumped, lost her grip, tripped, then stumbled out the gate and fell face first in the mud. Sil followed her out, stripping off her own helmet and goggles and buckling them to the rail. Crumble did the same, then closed the gate and made a wide lifting gesture. The bucket rose swiftly into the air, and the flier headed toward the port, the line and its cargo trailing behind it.

The silence, broken only by Pal's gulping breaths, was a

relief. Sil looked around at the hala trees, a few blooms just opening among the canopy, then down the scrubby hillside, across the valley toward town. They had three days of walking to convince Pal that she needed to stay and help stop the manifestation of the Uncaring God. All while trudging on non-existent trails, avoiding predators, and not freezing to death.

"Well." Sil watched Pal stagger to her feet, the front of her coated in a layer of mud and crushed greenery. "This ought to be fun."

PART III

*S*omewhat to Sil's surprise, the auto-pollinator did what it was supposed to.

"Can you see it? Where did it go?" Pal's mood had improved as soon as she had started working on the task at hand. She slid down the slope, catching herself on a clump of bluequince brambles. The smell of dried and mildewed berries wafted through the air. "There it is. It's going to another flower."

Sil observed from a more level spot. The machine flitted from branch to branch, then crawled inside unfurling petals and emerged again, pollen visible on the brush in the front. If nothing killed the trees in the meantime, by spring there should be more fruit ready to harvest. Then it would either rot on the ground or, more likely, as many low clan as could make the trip would hike out and gorge themselves on the fruit they could never afford.

Unlike most trees, hala weren't seasonal, producing both flowers and fruit all year long. That worried Sil a bit. This close to the edge of the non-terraformed expanse, it was more likely something on the heavily mutated planet would find this large and constant source of food. Sil suspected the birds would be the biggest beneficiaries, but if that brought in bigger predators, the colony might have a problem.

If that did happen, it would be easy enough to solve. None of the fruit produced viable seeds, a modification made by the designer so the trees couldn't propagate on their own. One person with a sharp knife could strip a ring of bark on all these trunks in a few days, assuming the hypothetical big predators didn't get that person first. Why would the colonists put up with additional risks when they weren't seeing any of the benefits? Whoever had planned this entire project hadn't understood the Jackpot Drift low clan at all.

And if the trees didn't start attracting predators, it wouldn't be long before someone uprooted one and moved it to a more convenient, and hidden, spot. When they got back to town, she would have to suggest it to Pyr. The trick was going to be making sure that not too many disappeared.

Crumble was following the buggy as it made switchbacks down the hill, but she knew him well enough to realize he was distracted by something. She left Pal to her attempts to record the auto-pollinator and climbed down to check on him.

"I keep hearing... echoes," he said when she had caught up. He tapped his head, where the scars were nearly hidden by his hair. "It must be some weird signal propagation, maybe something from town bouncing off the ionosphere. I can't make any of it out, but I think that's because I'm a little obsolete."

Their attempts to get Crumble's mech hardware upgraded kept getting blocked. He rarely let on how much it bothered him, but Sil knew it did. "We could always threaten to leave her out here on her own until she agrees to sort out the upgrades."

Drawn by the boundary center Sil had in her pocket, the

auto-pollinator moved to a closer tree, this one a modified fir. As she watched, the tiny machine flitted to a couple of branches and eventually decided the tree didn't match the parameters. It flew to the next tree and Sil relaxed. The identification module had been based on an off-planet tree database, because there wasn't one for Jackpot Drift. She'd been a little worried about the pollinator cozying up to some non-hala tree and refusing to leave.

Pal trailed behind, tripping over vegetation as she kept her gaze on the branches. She started sliding, then recovered on more stable footing. Sil turned her gaze to Crumble so she wouldn't feel compelled to offer advice on how to walk on an unpaved surface. She kept her voice low. "I thought we might have to load her down so we wouldn't get back too quickly, but now I'm starting to think we're going to have to keep an eye on her so she doesn't hurt herself."

Crumble grinned as he watched the governor. "I don't think she's ever been away from a city. It's kind of cute."

"It's a disaster waiting to happen." Sil thought about how much she'd learned since she left her first home. The army had known how to teach city-dwellers to survive in the wilderness. Sil had internalized that training, and then layered it with her knowledge of Jackpot Drift.

In contrast, Pal hadn't noticed the foxbear watching from the tree she was walking under. The foxbear was too small to be a threat, but if the governor hadn't seen the red fur against the grey tree bark, she would never notice any of the more camouflaged predators.

Pal scrambled to keep from falling, and ended up near the two of them, breathing heavily. "It looks like it's working, and I have documentation. Should we call the flier back now or are there other tests you need to run?"

"Crumble needs soil samples from further down the hill," Sil said. The more tired Pal was before she figured out the flier wasn't coming back for them, the shorter the inevitable fight. At least she hoped it would work like that. "And we should see what the pollinator does around different vegetation."

They followed the buggy downhill, Crumble in front, and Pal trailing behind, still watching the auto-pollinator.

After the third time Pal had bumped into her, Sil stopped and put a hand on her elbow. "You need to watch where you're putting your feet. There shouldn't be any poisonous snakes in this area, but there are a lot of animals that dig burrows. You could easily break your leg."

"But then I might lose track of the pollinator."

Sil unfastened her pocket, pulled out the boundary center device, and handed it to Pal. "Right now it's set to stay within a circle that goes from here to about that big rock. If you tap the end twice, the auto-pollinator will return to you. Don't lose that thing." Crumble might be able to connect and bring the tiny machine back, but if it went beyond his range, she'd be stuck trying to fabricate a new pollinator from scraps of colony leftovers, and the replacement would be ten times the size and more likely to tear off a branch than land on it.

Sil started walking again. The amount of stumbling and scrambling behind her lessened.

"Why did you pick this place?" Pal's voice was breathy, probably the higher gravity catching up to her. "It's very different from Cinnabar."

So Pal had heard their shared accent, too. Sil wasn't surprised. "The army promised a plot of land when I signed on, but they never specified where it would be." Back then, Sil's only thought had been to avoid forced labor or incarceration, but it still galled her she'd never thought to get the specifics. "When I got out, I had three choices, all of them bad, and Jackpot Drift seemed the least likely to kill me."

In fact, Jackpot Drift had merely been the farthest away

from the center of civilization. With the chaos godlet newly entrenched within her, she had been hoping for a place where nobody would notice if she did anything odd. Instead, everybody here noticed everything and accepted it. She'd been expecting a colony of loners with no families, but she'd found a community of people who formed their own. Somehow, she had been sucked into the middle of it. Sil still wasn't sure how that had happened.

A patch of darker brown by her boot caught her eye. Sil stopped and crouched so she could look at it more closely.

Pal stopped and leaned over. "What is it? Is it something dangerous?"

"That looks like goat poop." The pellets were dried out and scattered, but Sil had looked at a lot of goat droppings in the past year. "Weird." She stood up and started walking again. The prosthesis handled the terrain better than she had feared. She hadn't been able to ask the doctor about the hike; a secret only stayed a secret if nobody knew about it. Besides, she'd been pretty sure the doctor would have strong opinions about the idea, and Sil didn't want to listen to them.

"Why is that weird?"

"Because there aren't any goats out here. At least, none that I know of." She supposed there could be a herd, escapees from some farm who had traveled this direction and never been rounded up, but she wasn't seeing enough pellets for that. "Could be something else. Could be a lone goat that wandered off. If so, it's probably dead by now." She was a little surprised one goat would make it this far -- the nearest herd was just outside town and goats didn't like to be alone.

"I guess I understand how you ended up here, but how did you end up with sheep and goats?"

"And chickens," Sil added, glancing at Crumble. He and the couple Pyr had sent over to take care of the animals during their hike had spent a long time fussing over the chicks. Sil really hoped half of them weren't roosters. "Plus those useless horses Glass left behind, though hopefully we can get rid of them soon." She paused to look at some claw marks scratched into a tree. The bark had grown around the damage, so whatever had made it might have moved on. She hoped so.

"But surely you could have just worked as a nanotech. The One God knows, there's enough here that needs to be fixed."

"I didn't want to work for someone else. Especially not Glass." When Sil had arrived on Jackpot Drift, she'd been afraid to stay near people, worried that her chaos would either destroy something important, or be so recognizable a hunter would be called in. But she couldn't tell Pal that.

"Because of the chaos."

Adrenaline made Sil's hands tingle. Then she realized what the governor meant. Glass had ingested food infused with chaos, and a chaos hunter had taken him away. The entire colony had heard about the second part. If the hunters ever measured Glass for chaos again, he might be released, but until then he was stuck in whatever place they used to imprison people holding the older gods. "No. Because he was a jerk. I had enough of those telling me what to do in the army." She stopped and turned. "Is there some reason you're asking all these questions?"

"I can't just be curious?" Pal looked up. "Why isn't it moving?"

Sil followed Pal's line of sight and found the auto-pollinator sitting on a rock. "Probably recharging. We ran a lot of tests before we got here."

They reached the level ground between the hills. Ahead, Crumble had uncovered one corner of the tarp on the buggy and was using what looked like a dinner spoon to scrape some of the soil near the bluequince brambles into a jar. Sil rubbed at her face. If Pal had ever seen real soil sampling, Crumble's attempt to play the role would never work. Every so often, he would frown and glance around at signals only he could sense.

To keep Pal from noticing the farce ahead, Sil pointed to a notch cut at shoulder level on a fir tree. "That marks the trail you thought was a road. Keep following those and you'll eventually end up back in town." And that was exactly what they would be doing for the next few days, but Pal didn't know that yet.

"If I ever get stuck out here, I'm just going to sit down until someone comes for me." Pal looked at the tree, and then at Sil. "I know you think I just can't read a terrain display, but I'm telling you, these trails were clearly coded as improved roads." She frowned. "Why would someone falsify the data that way? That makes the wrong auto-pollinators look like less an oversight and more deliberate sabotage. But who would that benefit?"

Sil shrugged. "The tree growers?"

"No, it's going to take them years to fulfill the orders they already have. In fact, I was a little surprised the previous governor hadn't sold our allotment to someone lower on the list. That's what I would have done if I'd known the roads hadn't been built yet." She frowned. "This is a huge resource commitment, and without the infrastructure, it has no bene-fit. Why would someone want this colony to fail?"

"Even if they did, why would they need to do anything at all? The colony is well on its way to failing on its own." Sil leaned against the tree with the blaze showing the path back. Her head ached. "*Somebody* has to be getting something out of it."

Pal turned to look up the slope they had just covered, then back again. "Did the last governor just want a source of hala fruit for himself? Did he hike very often?"

The idea forced a laugh from Sil. "Rho never wanted to set foot on the planet if he could help it. Though I suppose he could have intended to send someone else to harvest them." Still, a whole grove seemed excessive, even for someone who cared as little for the colony's well-being as Rho.

Pal shook her head, as if to clear her mind. "I'll open an inquiry when I get back. I guess the trees aren't going anywhere now, but maybe the next governor can get a settlement for the colony if there is evidence of fraud somewhere." She raised her voice so Crumble would hear. "I've seen enough. Call the flier back and let's get out of here."

In a quieter voice she added, "One God's blessing, I'm going to have to get back in that contraption again, aren't I?"

Sil sat down and slouched against the tree, which had a gently sloping trunk perfect for that purpose. "Wake me up when it gets here." The relief that went through her when she closed her eyes was so intense she almost didn't decipher Pal's irritated query to Crumble.

"What is *wrong* with her?"

The sunlight slanted more sharply when Sil opened her eyes again. She was propped against something lumpy -- camping supplies, unless she missed her guess -- but she was comfortably warm. For a moment she considered dropping back to sleep, but Pal spoke.

"Why haven't they arrived yet? It's been hours. Signal them again." She was pacing, arms wrapped around herself.

"I'll try, but nobody's responding. Maybe our ship comm is broken." Crumble banged the box against the ground and clicked it on again. Since the "ship comm" was actually an obsolete short range communicator whose interior had succumbed to the elements long ago, Sil wasn't surprised when his next transmission received no response. He noticed Sil stirring and smiled at her. "Welcome back."

Sil stood up, absently folding the sleeping bag that had been draped over her. "Sorry. It just sort of came over me."

Crumble waved her words away and took the sleeping bag to stow in the buggy. "Not a problem. We haven't been able to contact the flicr to come pick us up again, so it's not like there was anything else to do."

Sil wished she'd stayed asleep longer. "Still? Is the ship comm broken?" She winced as the words came out. She was terrible at acting. Even a small child would sound more plausible.

Pal stared at her, brow furrowed, but then she seemed to dismiss Sil and turned back to Crumble. "But even if they don't hear from us, they'll come back and look, won't they?"

"I think so." Crumble fiddled with the button on the communicator. "Zoom Zoom Room or crew, come in, please. This is the ground party."

Sil resisted the urge to groan. Crumble wasn't any better at lying than she was. They should have had Mer with them. Mer would have intimidated Pal into not asking questions. Except Mer couldn't have made the three-day hike back to town without assistance.

Sil wished she'd just let Mer shove Pal into a stasis box for a few days. Sure, they had a failure rate that really only made them acceptable to use in emergencies, but chances were high that Pal wouldn't have died, and Sil wouldn't be out here trying to convince the colony's governor she had no idea what was going on.

"You *think* so?" Pal's voice had gained an edge. "There's not a backup plan?"

Crumble shrugged. "We're only a couple days away from town if we walk. We have supplies if we need to do that."

"A couple days..." Pal strode forward and grabbed the communicator. "Ship's crew, this is Governor Palladium Riversedge. Respond immediately." She waited. When there was not even static, she pounded the heel of her hand against the communicator. With an audible crack, the casing split open, releasing a pile of rusted metal and warped plastic from the interior.

All three of them stared at the detritus lying on top of dirt and leaves.

Crumble was the first to respond. "Oops."

Sil cleared her throat. "Nice job. You broke the communicator."

That got a twitch of a smile from Crumble, but Pal wheeled to face her. "You! You did this!" She threw the remains of the communicator in her hand at Sil, but her aim was so far off that Sil didn't even bother to duck. "On purpose!" She seemed to be having difficulty coming up with words.

Sil looked at Crumble. "Why is she blaming me? Everyone knows you're the sneakier one, don't they?"

Crumble tugged on one earlobe. "I have a theory."

"One God's toenails, we're not back at the interesting ears thing, are we? Because I might have to take another nap, if you're bringing that up again."

Pal had found her voice, and her volume. "You! You're never happy until you've ruined things for *everyone*."

"I'm not?" Sil thought back. "Is this about the roads? Because I *told* you there weren't any roads out here." Granted, she did have a lot of disasters to her credit, even from before the chaos godlet had joined her, but Jackpot Drift had so many disasters -- she didn't see why Pal would single her out when there were so many other things to blame.

"Of course it's not about the roads. You've been ruining things for me my entire life!"

Sil stopped and squinted at the governor. "We just met a few weeks ago. Are you sure you're not mistaking me for someone else?" She glanced at Crumble as another thought occurred. "She didn't hit her head when we landed, did she?" They'd been wearing helmets, so it seemed unlikely, but if Pal was having a medical emergency, they were in trouble. All they had was a basic first aid kit, and help was three days away.

Crumble glanced around, as if trying to find the source of

a sound. "This would be so much easier if you people gave your children more sensible names. But instead, everybody ends up with the same name, so none of them means anything at all."

Pal was still focused on Sil. "You destroy things and you don't even notice who gets hurt in the process! Then you just go on with your life and leave everyone else to pick up the pieces." She threw up her hands and stomped up the hill.

Sil moved closer to Crumble and watched her go. "Her entire life? I don't think I even knew any high clan on Cinnabar. She must have the wrong person."

"You knew one high clan. At least, your mother did." Crumble stopped trying to find the source of the signal and turned his attention fully on her. "You people use matrilineal surnames. My people name children after the father, or the presumed father anyhow, except when the child is brought up by the temple."

Having had exposure to the way Crumble's mind worked, Sil saw where he was heading with this conversation. "That's not possible."

"Isn't it? I did a little digging back when she first got here. Both of you list a father called Tellurium, but since that's in the top three most common names, I wanted to get confirmation before I said anything. You told me you never met your father's high clan family. If you didn't meet them, why would you remember their names?" He smoothed her hair back behind one ear. "And she has the same ears."

Sil frowned and shook her hair back down. "It's not possible." It absolutely *was* possible. She had known she had half-siblings somewhere, but she'd never imagined meeting them. "But even if that's true, shouldn't she be mad at her father? Why me? What did I do..." Sil trailed off as she remembered the events that had made her leave Cinnabar City.

"If I remember correctly, you said there was something

about salting words into the grass on his estate so they could be seen from a distance?"

"But... They *had* to have known about my mother and me. And I was just trying to embarrass *him*." Her father had made promises for years about raising Sil and her mother up to the high clan.

Sil had stopped believing him about the time she noticed how common that trope was in the daily serials, but her mother kept insisting it was only a matter of time. Her mother had worked to change both their accents, and complained that her relatives were too common. Sil's childhood had been lonely by low clan standards; her mother had been so obsessed with trying to join the high clan she'd never noticed she'd abandoned what benefits she'd been born with.

Crumble touched her arm. "That may have been your intent, but it sounds like that may not have been the outcome."

"But it was half a lifetime ago." Sil gestured to their surroundings. "And it's not like I made her come to Jackpot Drift."

"True, but you were there when the One God first spoke through her." He held up a hand to forestall her protest. "I know you had nothing to do with that, but she may not be thinking too clearly. And you did just help strand her on the planet for at least the next few weeks."

Sil watched Pal trying to climb the hill. The governor followed a groove worn into the earth by runoff instead of using the longer route where shrubs and other plants had stabilized the surface. Every few steps, she slid backward again. It looked like something Sil's chaos would have instigated, but the cat remained quiet. "Is she planning on going up there and waving her arms around or something? She can't think the ship in orbit is going to notice her."

"I think she's too angry to have a plan." Crumble handed

Sil the sleeping bag he still held. "Can you repack the buggy while I talk her down? We should be able to travel another hour before we lose the light." He trotted up the slope.

Sil pulled the tarp off the buggy. There was no need to hide the contents now. It looked like Crumble had been using the sleeping bag to cushion the jar of Pyr's finest distilled liquor. That must have been a last-minute addition. She checked to see that the stopper was secure, then wrapped the sleeping bag around it again.

She had a *sister* on Jackpot Drift. Palladium Riversedge was her *sister*. She tried that sentence in her head a few times, then snorted. No. A sister was someone you grew up with, related by blood or not. Palladium Riversedge was just someone who shared some common DNA. There was a big gap between the two.

Having resolved the issue to her own satisfaction, Sil loaded the rest of the camping gear she'd been sleeping on and replaced the tarp on the buggy. Eventually Pal would accept she was stuck here, and then they were going to have a long walk ahead of them.

o: Senior Agent Mercury Sweetair, eyes only

ANALYSIS OF SITE 1 IS CURRENTLY AWAITING FINALIZATION AND approval for distribution. Due to staffing constraints, no estimated date can be determined. The situation on Jackpot Drift appears urgent enough that I am authorizing limited dissemination of this preliminary analysis.

(SIGNED)
 Lapis Purpratum
 (Acting) Assistant Deputy Director
 Department of Forensic Investigation

PRELIMINARY FORENSIC REPORT ON SITE 1, JACKPOT DRIFT:

. . .

SEVEN BLOCKS OF EXPLOSIVES (SEE MAP) FAILED TO DETONATE within the underground site when the hatch was opened.

Rooms 1 and 2 were consistent with living quarters for long-term residents. DNA was recovered from 27 individuals.

Room 3 held equipment related to genetic modification and medium-sized species incubation.

Room 4 and 5 had connections expected for one AI each.

Room 6 held 30 cages, with evidence of recent use. No intact specimens, dead or alive, were found within site 1.

A SWEEP OF THE AREA WITHIN A RADIUS OF TWO KILOMETERS led to the discovery of human remains. Predation and decay make determining cause of death unlikely. Two distinct DNA sequences were recovered.

DNA FROM 6 OF THE 27 SAMPLES FROM ROOMS 1 & 2 matched humans detained on the ship *Star Slinger*. 2 samples matched the bodies found outside the site. The remaining 19 samples are unidentified.

SUBJECTIVE ANALYSIS:

The detonation failure appears to have been caused by the corrosive nature of the local environment. We believe the explosives were indeed meant to destroy the underground base.

Approximately 30% of the equipment in room 3 was non-functional, bolstering the theory that increased oxidation due to high concentrations of sulfur and other oxidizers in the immediate vicinity were an ongoing problem.

The scattering of human remains found outside site 1 makes it impossible to definitively state that only two bodies were present. Body #1 shows evidence of generalized bone remodeling, consistent with degenerative joint disease. Body #2 shows more mild changes. No attempt appeared to have been made to bury or hide the remains that were found, so it is likely the unknown 19 humans left site 1 earlier.

Room 4 appeared to have had an AI connected until recently. Room 5 did not appear to have been used.

DNA recovered from cages in room 6 do not match any known organism. Closest relation: flittermouse, with sequences that may have been copied from dorral, sandcat, and human, among others. (Expected appearance based on DNA reconstruction attached.)

INTEGRATED ANALYSIS:

At least one AI and up to 19 humans escaped the raids in the system. Site 1 had been evacuated about one colony day before it was breached, which suggests prior knowledge of the raid.

Given all available evidence, it is likely the modified organisms held in the cages were created specifically to become the host of the Uncaring God during its manifestation. It remains unknown whether those organisms were removed from the system or remain in a different location on the planet.

RECOMMENDATIONS:

Recovery and destruction of the created organisms should be the major priority, along with quarantine of the unknown AI and remaining humans from the site.

Because it is possible the organisms had left the system before the raid, evacuation and sterilization of the planet of Jackpot Drift is not recommended at this time.

*P*al walked in stoney silence as they made their way along the trail in the dying light. The buggy bounced around at the front of their line, followed by Sil, and then Pal. Crumble brought up the rear. Sil was impressed he could drive the buggy and pay attention to where he was walking, but he didn't seem to have any problem with it.

She was considering whether she should call for a rest break when the buggy stopped. The area was level enough to sleep, wasn't so close to the stream that a sudden burst of rain would cause flooding, and didn't appear to be on any animal path that would bring them into contact with dangerous predators. When she turned, Crumble indicated he was going to look around the area, and he headed off the trail when she gestured assent. Then Sil looked at Pal.

The governor had the blank stare of someone who had passed her limit and was just trying to keep up. Sil recognized it from the face of all the exhausted new recruits she'd seen over the years. Maybe the governor's silence hadn't been entirely due to anger after all. When she had repacked the buggy, Sil had noticed a stash of sweet pastries. Now she dug one out, split it, and handed half to Pal. "A little sugar will help."

Startled out of her stupor, Pal looked like she was going to argue for an instant, but then she grabbed it from Sil and took a bite. "I should never have come here."

Sil didn't pause in her search for the sheep jerky buried deeper in their supplies. "You wouldn't be the first person to say that." Her fingers hit the container she'd been looking for and she pushed it in Pal's direction. "Have a piece of this." She set up the camp stove and started heating water.

Crumble appeared when the tea had finished brewing. He took the cup Sil offered and stood next to her by the buggy. "If I were still in the army, I'd think someone had a base set up near here and I was picking up on signal leakage." He looked at Pal, who was staring into space, tea in one hand and half-eaten jerky in the other. "How are things going?"

"About like you'd expect." Sil held the jerky container toward him. "I think we should plan on camping here tonight so nobody falls off a cliff because they're too tired to care."

"That works for me." He looked at the trunks of the fir trees where there were horizontal scars in the bark at waist height. "Is the thing leaving those likely to be a problem?"

"No." Back on her farm in the hills, Sil had seen the shy omnivores that made those marks. "It will avoid the area until we're gone." She thought for a moment. "Signal leakage?"

"Maybe. I'd swear on your One God's left hangnail that there's something there."

Sil gave an involuntary snort at the profanity spoken with Crumble's Oldlander accent. "I don't think there are any farms out here. So I doubt an AI would have moved here."

"I agree. But there's at least one AI on the planet with a

self-powered vehicle. It's studying different mutations in the fish population."

"Fish?"

"Fish. In the ocean. I don't get the appeal either, but the AIs were very excited about it all. Anyhow, I could be picking up something from it if it's close enough."

"Can you determine the direction? We should check it out." Right after she said it, Sil shook her head and smiled ruefully. "Too long in the army, sorry. For all we know, it's something the tree-planting crews left behind that hasn't lost power yet. What else would be out here?"

"If it's something they left behind, it's fair game, right? It might be worth coming out here again in spring to see if it's anything we can use. Assuming I can find it again. The transmissions are so short I can't lock down where it's coming from." Crumble crouched by the buggy. "How does noodle soup sound for dinner?"

———

IN THE MIDDLE OF THE NIGHT, THE ONLY THING SIL COULD feel was the warmth of Crumble's legs against her back. Everything else had gone numb. The sleeping bag kept her just warm enough that she didn't need to shiver, but the night had turned cold, the way early winter occasionally did. She took comfort that the plunging temperatures meant the skies were clear and they wouldn't be breaking through drifts of snow the next day.

Next to her Crumble was seated, his back against one of the fir trees, cocooned in his own sleeping bag. On his other side, she could hear Pal's rhythmic breathing.

Sil rolled over and gave up on sleeping for the moment. "See anything out there?" Crumble would be using the night vision camera on the buggy. She kept her voice low, though she suspected Pal wouldn't wake up unless someone shouted at her.

"Some large birds and a lot of rodents." Crumble kept his voice quiet as well. "I never realized so many animals were around at night. Especially towards winter."

A mink chattered in the distance. Sil let her thoughts drift. "What are the chances that Captain Idiot is asleep on our bed?"

"Without you there? Probably very low." Crumble unfastened his sleeping bag enough that he could reach out and brush Sil's hair back from her face. "It really is beautiful out here."

"Very romantic," Sil mumbled.

"You, me... the stars."

"The mud. The freezing temperature... my half-sister." Sil reached up and threaded her fingers through his, though it made her exposed flesh burn from the cold. She felt him laugh.

"Ah, well, we'll have to work on it." He squeezed her hand, then let go. She heard his sleeping bag rustle again as he refastened it. "You should get some rest..." His voice trailed off.

Then he was speaking at a normal volume. "There's something happening. The signal leakage... There's definitely at least one AI out here."

At the same time, a glow filled the campsite. Sil struggled to get out of her sleeping bag while the impossibly musical voice of the One God spoke from Pal's mouth. "*The paths are open. The way is hard, but the paths are open.*"

Crumble got to his feet, ducking around trees to look into the darkness. He concentrated on one spot, on a line perpendicular to the path back to town.

Sil finally wriggled free from the sleeping bag and yanked on her boots. Her chaos cat stirred. Sil hoped it wasn't about to go another round with the One God, but it seemed more watchful than anything else. Whatever was happening out there, the chaos godlet wasn't happy about it.

Pulling the sleeping bag around her shoulders, Sil leaned toward Crumble. The unknown AI activating at the same time the One God showed up couldn't be a coincidence. "Can you tell where it's coming from?" She had to yell to be heard above the One God's words, which were now just the same sentence over and over.

"*The way is hard, but the paths are open.*"

Crumble closed his eyes and pointed with his chin. "Over there."

With her good leg, Sil drew a line in the mud parallel to his motion. "Any sense of how far away?"

Crumble wrapped his sleeping bag around her. "Stay here and take care of your sister. I'll try to get a second point for triangulation." He trotted into the darkness, without a light or the coat currently under Pal.

"Stupid Oldlander is going to freeze to death," she grumbled. "And she's not my sister."

"*The way is hard, but the paths are open. The way is hard, but the--*"

Sil frowned at her One God-taken half-sister, whose face was too bright to look at directly. "We got that part. Can you try saying something useful for a change?"

"*... is hard, but the paths are open.*"

And then, just as suddenly as it had appeared, the One God retreated, leaving Sil blind in the darkness. She waited, listening for movement, as her night vision slowly came back. Pal's breathing returned to a deep and even rhythm. The normal sounds of the night replaced the silence. By the time Crumble jogged back, Sil could see the white plumes of his breath in the light of the stars.

"I lost the signal right about the time the camp stopped glowing." He took the sleeping bag Sil handed him, and they started bedding down again. "If I did my math correctly, we're about five kilometers away. More or less."

Sil paused in crawling into her bag and stared into the darkness, letting her memory fill in the details. "At least beyond that hill then." It wasn't on their path; none of the hala fruit trees had been planted over there, and it was outside the range of the marked trail.

Part of her wanted to go find the site right away, but then what? Sil and Crumble had been soldiers, but they had no weapons with them and no backup. Pal, unfamiliar with Jackpot Drift or camping during winter, couldn't be left to find her own way back. "We need to get back and tell Mer. We'll just have to hope they don't succeed in manifesting the Uncaring God for another few days."

Crumble hummed agreement.

On the other side of Crumble, Pal started snoring. Despite it all, or maybe because of it, Sil snickered.

Crumble inched closer in his sleeping bag. "Very romantic."

Sil rolled her eyes but let herself relax against his warmth as they both stared out into the deceptively quiet night.

tatus report from Senior Agent Mercury Sweetair:

Initial draft (unsent):

Updates:

Thank you for the preliminary forensic report on Site 1.

Please see attached information linking flittermice to hala trees, along with incomplete financial information about the hala trees recently imported to Jackpot Drift.

Analysis:

It would have been useful to know the AIs were modifying flittermice -- mammals that eat hala blossoms -- as vessels for the Uncaring God *before* I sent the new governor on a tour of the recently planted and mysteriously funded hala trees just to keep her from leaving the system.

Now I find out I may have sent our only speaker for the One God to the most likely spot of the AI conspiracy. Worse,

I've sent her with the two people most likely to blow everything up in the process.

This literally could not have been more badly planned.

Now I need to go out there and try to salvage the situation. One God's nose hairs, you people are going to be the death of me.

FINAL DRAFT:

Updates: Financial transactions regarding hala trees (attached) considered suspicious and require further investigation.

Analysis: Strong possibility revival of AI conspiracy is centered near attached coordinates. Mobilizing now for reconnaissance and possible intervention. Urgent assistance required.

28

*R*elaxed and comfortable in the pre-dawn blackness, Sil considered staying just a few more minutes to enjoy the warmth from being sandwiched between... Her eyes flew open. Crumble was in front of her, but there was someone behind her. Pal's audible breathing from beyond Crumble proved it wasn't her. Sil rolled onto her back and quietly unfastened her sleeping bag. If she needed to fight, she wanted her arms clear.

A tongue scraped along her exposed knuckles. If the gesture hadn't been so familiar, she would have screamed. As it was, she reached out further and found the horns she thought she would find, automatically scratching the nearby poll.

Sil elbowed Crumble and waited for his breathing to change. "Why is there a goat next to me?"

His voice was full of sleep when he finally answered. "Is that some sort of theological question?" His laugh broke off when she elbowed him again. "Nothing about the One God you people worship has ever made any sense to me." He laughed again. "The goat came by a few hours ago, and it seemed to recognize you. No, it's not Captain Idiot," he said quickly as she drew in a breath.

Of course, it wasn't Captain Idiot. All of Sil's goats were too far away to suddenly show up in the middle of the night. She considered getting up, but really, there was nothing to do until it got lighter. Pal was asleep on Sil's coat, anyway. Awake enough to recognize that for the rationalization that it was, Sil refastened her sleeping bag and enjoyed being warm.

Once it got light enough to move around without walking into gullies, they needed to get moving. The sooner they got back to town with their news, the better their chances of taking down the conspiracy before the Uncaring God manifested and broke the universe.

But getting lost or injured would slow them down more than resting until daylight. The best part of considering their safety was that she didn't need to get out of her warm sleeping bag at the moment. She fell asleep again while congratulating herself on having both warmth and a plan.

*C*rumble shook her awake what felt like seconds later. But the red light of dawn suffused the campsite, which meant it had been hours.

"Pal's gone."

The words took a moment to make sense. Then she flipped over to look at Pal's definitely empty sleeping bag. "How? When?" Crumble had his coat on, but Sil's still lay near Pal's spot. Pal's coat and boots were missing. "Did she leave intentionally, or do you think she got lost out there?" Sil pulled on her boots and fastened them.

"I heard her go, but I thought she just needed to find a tree. And then I didn't really worry about how long she was taking because she had that sheep jerky. You know what that can do to a person who isn't used to it." Crumble picked up Sil's coat and held it up for her to pull on. "By the time I got worried and thought to look, I couldn't find her."

"She wouldn't be stupid enough to think she could outrun us to town, would she?" Sil dismissed the idea even as she said it. Pal was angry about missing her berth on the outgoing transport, but she had been exhausted the night before and would undoubtedly be sore this morning. She also would be smart enough to take the lightweight sleeping bag, even if she thought she could go two days without any other supplies. "She still has the control in her coat, so the pollinator should follow her. Can you connect to it?"

Crumble closed his eyes, then rotated to point in the direction where the signal had been coming from the night before. "Over there." He opened his eyes.

Sil blew out a breath. "The One God must be doing something."

"If we hurry, maybe we'll be able to catch her before she gets herself into trouble."

With a glance at the goat grazing nearby, Sil stowed her sleeping bag and Crumble did the same. A cold miserable hike back to town was only going to be worse if the goat ate their bedding. Sil pulled out food to eat on the move. The water in her flask was cold, just barely warm enough to drink, but at least it hadn't frozen solid.

Crumble led her to the spot where he'd last seen Pal, but Sil could have found it on her own, almost as quickly. Her half-sister hadn't made any attempt to disguise her trail. Possibly she didn't even know she was making a trail, or how to avoid it. In any case, Sil caught sight of the boot prints in the mud and over frozen grass.

The tracks led in a straight line up the next hill, evidence the One God was guiding Pal. Ideally, Sil and Crumble would have taken the faster route around the base, but they didn't know the area and Sil didn't want to risk losing the trail. They followed the uneven boot prints uphill.

Sil's lower back ached before they were halfway there. The sun was heating the ground, loosening the mud that had still been frozen when Pal had gone over it not too long before. As she gritted her teeth and accepted Crumble's help over a fallen tree, an unrelated puzzle worked itself out in Sil's brain.

"She's one of Captain Idiot's kids," Sil panted as they trudged up the hill. "She had twins and one of them disappeared right about the time they were weaning. I assumed it was carried off and eaten." No wonder the goat had recognized her. She'd been born on Sil's bed, and Sil had handled her daily.

"Carried off, then," Crumble said, "but somehow not eaten."

They kept walking.

"Pal can't possibly be too far ahead of us," Sil said. She unfastened her coat and loosened her scarf. "She was struggling on hills yesterday, and she *has* to be sore today."

"I think we would have caught up to her already if she'd been the one making decisions." Crumble stopped before they got to the top of the hill. "But the One God doesn't strike me as the kindest of gods."

Sil's chaos godlet knocked a dead branch off a nearby tree in agreement.

Sil touched Crumble's shoulder to get his attention and gestured at a clump of shrubs on their right that went over the top of the hill. The greenery would be harder to move through, but they could look at what was on the other side of the hill without being silhouetted for anyone looking from below.

More bluequince brambles caught at her coat and the powdered berries disintegrated in the air around them as they climbed up. When they reached the crest, Sil crouched and looked down.

Pal was limping down the face of the hill, and for a moment Sil didn't notice anything else. She was about to get up and chase after her half-sister when Crumble put a hand on her shoulder.

"Down there." He pointed. "They're camouflaged, but there are a couple of shelters."

Sil looked in the direction he was pointing, and finally saw them on the opposite hill face. Fabricated structures similar to her old cabin, they had been placed in such a way that they were hidden from above, and the colors had been chosen to blend in with the area. They had been further obscured by a layer of mud and old branches.

Overall, it was a decent effort, but it looked like a rushed job, nonetheless. With the way the hills came together, Sil was fairly certain at least one of the three buildings would be carried off by heavy rains in spring. It was already missing support under one corner.

Pal was heading straight toward the buildings, picking up speed as gravity helped her along.

Sil blew out a breath. "There's no way they don't see her, unless they aren't looking at all." She turned her head to look at Crumble. "Do we risk exposing all three of us and grab her now, or wait to see what happens?"

Crumble frowned at the scene before them. "Will the One God even let us interfere? She's moving like it's still in control." He ducked his head to look around a branch. "They must not have anybody on watch."

Their eyes met, and they both stood up.

Bits of dried bluequince brambles clung to Sil as she hurried down the slope, Crumble at her side.

"I always have the most fun when I'm around you." He leapt over a fallen branch.

"Are you still trying to convince me this is a romantic trip?"

They had almost reached Pal, but they were also nearly at the buildings. This close, it was more obvious the structures didn't belong. From the way the surrounding branches showed early signs of recovering, the buildings might have been there since the middle of summer.

Sil moved to the side, planning to herd her sister the same way she herded the sheep when they got out. With the One God controlling her, Pal might be just as dangerous. There was no point wasting energy going back over the top of the hill; if they followed the gully to the side, eventually they'd be close to their camp.

"Ahead," Crumble warned. "I count four people. No, five."

Bundled up against the cold, a group of strangers came around the side of the middle building and hurried down the path connecting it to the structure below. They were watching Pal and yelling to each other.

Sil swore under her breath.

For just a second, she considered trying to bluff her way out of the situation. Maybe she could convince these people they were just on a hike. In early winter. With the One God's light blazing from Pal's face.

Then the man at the front of the group lifted a shotgun. Sil tackled her sister. "Down!"

The blast deafened her. From the corner of her eye, she saw Crumble hit the ground hard. He didn't move.

Terror spiked through her, followed by grief. Stupid mechs were never brought into battle for a reason -- they had no sense of self-preservation. Anger overwhelmed her. She was going to burn this place to the ground and salt the One God pissed-upon ashes. The chaos godlet within her moved.

For the first time, Sil urged it on.

With a low crunch, the valley jolted. Sil felt more than heard the crack of instacrete as the unsupported corner of the building failed. All five people facing her turned, even the man with the shotgun. As Sil watched, the unstable building split open, a third of it dropping away and rolling down the hill. Chunks of insulation and instacrete cartwheeled off to the sides.

A few grey *things* -- Sil's brain refused to label them birds -- about half her height came out, awkwardly flapping their wings and screeching. Two of them tumbled to the ground, wings tangled, but one caught an updraft and careened around, out of control but testing the currents. More of the grey animals came to the edge of the building, and two more leaped into the air.

All five of the strangers reversed course and ran toward the building, waving their arms and flapping jackets, trying to keep any more of the animals from escaping. More people came running out of the top building, coatless and bare-headed.

The part of Sil's brain that had carried her through a lifetime in the army took over. She would invade the lower building while they were distracted. Something in there would be useful as a weapon. Even if there wasn't, she had a pocketknife and years of training. All three buildings would be in flames before she was done. The man with the shotgun would be the first to drop.

She would make him wish he had never been born.

Farther down the slope, Crumble coughed and rolled to his feet. "We should probably get going."

Sil's focus changed so quickly, it made her head hurt. "You're... I thought you were dead." She looked him over as he stood up. Other than grass stains and new mud on top of old dirt, he seemed unchanged.

He reached down to take one of Pal's arms. "I told you the day we met -- I learned to duck. And I'm pretty lucky at not getting shot."

Sil reordered her priorities. If she wasn't going to slaughter all those strangers, the three of them needed to get away. Sil checked her sister. Pal's face wasn't glowing, so Sil assumed the One God was no longer in residence, but she looked confused. And cold. Sil shouldered the arm Crumble wasn't holding. "One, two, *three*." They hoisted Pal up to her feet and started jogging away, Pal trying to stagger along, but mostly hanging limply between them.

Another crash sounded behind them. Sil stole a look over her shoulder and saw the rest of the building canting toward its fallen corner, more animals flying from the opening. She faced forward again, gritted her teeth, and kept running. "We need to get out of sight," she said, timing her words with her breathing. At some point, the people behind them were going to have contained all the animals that could be gathered, and then she was pretty sure they were going to come after the three of them. The strangers were far better armed.

"I have a plan."

"Great." As they followed a stream bed in a curve around the hill, Sil glanced back. The buildings were no longer in sight, and she couldn't see any of the strangers. "I need to slow down." Her prosthesis felt like something might have broken when she'd dived to the ground, and she was having to pick that leg up higher than the other to keep from tripping.

They slowed to a walk. Pal's chin dropped to her chest, but her legs were still moving as if she were trying to help support her weight. After waiting a few seconds, Sil angled her head so she could see Crumble's face. "You had a plan?"

"Don't worry. It's in motion. Might be a few minutes though."

Sil tried to get her breath to even out. "I'll try not to get shot before then."

"Please."

The uneven ground slowed them further. Just when Sil thought she was going to have to call for a stop, the crackling of branches ahead made her drop Pal's arm and leap to the side. If their attackers had somehow managed to get in front of them, spreading out would make it more likely someone might get in close enough to grab the shotgun.

Crumble lowered Pal down to a sitting position, but didn't leave her. "It's okay. This is my plan."

A goat's head emerged from a clump of bushes. The doe that had kept Sil warm the night before trotted out. Sil looked from Crumble to the goat and then back again. "*This* is your plan?"

"No, that's a goat." He gestured beyond the goat and the buggy came forward. "*That* is my plan."

Sil nodded. "That's a better plan." She helped him remove the packs and the sleeping bags from the buggy, and then they lifted Pal onto it. As long as Pal was awake enough to keep from falling off, this would work. One of the sleeping bags went around her shoulders, and then they started moving again.

*J*t wasn't until Sil had let herself collapse in the same spot they'd spent the night that she realized why her prosthesis had started moving so oddly.

"One God's nose hairs," she swore as she looked at the holes in her leggings. "I got hit." She poked her finger through the cloth and into the interior of the prosthesis. The pellets hadn't gone all the way through, but they had disrupted some of the mechanics.

"You really are hard on those things." Crumble handed her a cup of cold-brewed tea and a handful of jerky.

He'd given the last of the pastries to Pal, coaxing her to eat. Sil's half-sister was a little more aware of her surroundings, and she'd mumbled a thank you to Crumble when he'd given her tea, but she still looked like she might fall over at any second. They'd wrapped her in all three sleeping bags and propped her up against a tree. Sil's attempts to convince the goat to sit down next to Pal had failed until she'd sat down nearby. Now the goat was lying between them.

Crumble spoke around a mouthful of food. "What were those flying things?"

Sil stopped jabbing her fingers into the prosthesis and smoothed out the fabric on top. "Nothing I've ever seen on Jackpot Drift before." She drank more tea while she thought about it. "Remember the flittermice I asked Mer to look out for? They look a little like that. Not nearly as big as these ones, though. They had equipment for genetic manipulation stored in the post office. Now I think we know why."

"And why the hala trees were imported." Crumble dug the medical kit from his bag and sat in front of Sil. "Can I see?"

Sil gave him a quizzical look. "You realize the prosthesis isn't alive, right? I mean, I know you liked to carry on conversations with the last one, but..." When he held out his hand, she stretched out her leg so he could look.

He pulled her leggings out of the way so he could see the damage. "I'm not worried about infection, obviously, but it's not waterproof any more. If you get leaves and dirt inside, it's going to stop moving completely." He felt along the length of it for any other damage, then bent to peer at the pellet holes. "I should be able to cover the defects with bandages and tissue glue. It might be better to get the pellets out first, but I don't see them." He waved away her pantomimed suggestions she could remove the prosthesis to make it easier for him. "This is fine."

Sil relaxed for the first time since she'd woken up, letting the warmth given off by the goat seep in. Something about the way one stranger had moved nagged at her.

"I've never had anybody crack a building in half for me before." Crumble's voice was quiet as he worked with the acrid glue, and he didn't look up at her.

Sil felt her face flush. "I thought you were dead." She blew out a breath. "I was ready to rush in there like an idiot, armed with a tiny folding knife, just to make them sorry. My drill instructors must be looking down at me in shame." She shrugged. "Assuming they're dead, of course."

"It's just that I'm not sure how I'll ever top that."

"Why would you want to?" She took another sip of tea. "Are we having some sort of contest to see who can do the stupidest thing? You should have told me earlier. I have untapped depths."

Crumble smiled and shifted her leg a little so he could work on a different spot. "I've never seen it on a list of the most romantic things to do for your partner, but I think that's just because most people don't have the opportunity."

Sil lowered the tea and jerky to the ground. "Are you serious?" He was. She could see it in his face, in every muscle of the body she'd come to know so well. "You've been taking care of me for weeks. I've never heard you complain once, not even when I fell asleep and nearly destroyed the kitchen. Every step of the way, you've just been *there*. Just because you're you." She raised her tea up to her mouth again. "Me losing my mind and trying to burn down the world doesn't even rank."

Crumble's eyes flicked up and *looked* at her. He leaned forward. Sil's blood heated, mud or no mud.

Pal's voice cut through the air. "I was supposed to *kill* those things. And you set them all free!"

Crumble rocked back with a laugh. Sil sighed and looked at her sister. "You walked straight into their camp and nearly got all of us killed."

Pal opened her mouth as if she were going to argue, then a look of confusion passed over her face. "I did, didn't I. I don't..." She stopped, then started again. "I got up to go to the bathroom, and then I recognized the way I needed to go, and..."

Sil and Crumble waited.

Pal rubbed at her face. "It never occurred to me to come back and wake you, or to wait and see if anyone was around. I just kept walking, and then I saw the building, and then I just knew I had to go in there and kill everything."

Pulling the sleeping bags more tightly around her shoulders, she shook her head. "That's not right. We need to go back to town so they can put me in a stasis chamber until they figure out what is wrong with me. I could have killed someone." Her voice had grown decisive during the last part, a high clan governor telling two people, one low clan and the other an Oldlander, what to do. She sat up straighter. "Why is there a goat here?"

Sil bristled at her sister's tone, but subsided when Crumble put a hand on her good leg. His voice was level. "Do you remember anything that happened last night?"

Pal cocked her head. "I remember... going to bed and thinking everything hurt too much to sleep. And then it was morning."

Crumble nodded. "I thought that might be the case." He gave her a summary of the attempted manifestation as he continued to patch the hole in Sil's prosthesis. "I think your One God decided to hurry things along this morning."

Pal absorbed the news in silence for a few moments. "So you're saying that they almost manifested the Uncaring God last night, and now, instead of all of those animals being in one place where we could get rid of them at once, they're scattered all over the valley."

Sil liked Crumble's view of the building collapse better than Pal's. "If *we* can't get to those flittermouse-things, neither can they. And it's not like this planet is friendly to new wildlife. The way those things were moving around, it didn't look like they'd ever been out of a cage before. My guess is they'll be dinner for something else by the end of the week."

Pal wasn't deterred. "But we'll have no way of knowing if they're all gone. You should have killed them first before destroying the building." She stopped and looked confused again. "And how did you destroy the building? I didn't see any explosives. And you wouldn't have had a chance to put them there."

Sil looked at Crumble. "That... wasn't really our doing."

Pal frowned at her. "I'm not an idiot. The building didn't suddenly fall apart when someone was shooting at us..." She trailed off, then looked at Crumble in horror. "You're an Oldlander. You did it with one of the older gods, didn't you? You have chaos!" She got to her feet, as if she were going to run.

Sil waved. "Actually, that would be me." When Crumble opened his mouth, she glared at him. "Hush."

Crumble ignored her. "I have luck. She has chaos."

So much for trying to keep him safe. Sil raised an eyebrow at her sister. "And we're at least two days away from anybody else who can help you, so you might want to rethink some things." She huffed a laugh. "Plus, you ended up with the One God, who almost got us all killed this morning, so you don't have the high ground here. Sit your god-chosen butt back down and listen."

Crumble's shoulders shook, but he went back to patching the damage.

Pal considered for a moment, then sat down again. "I thought a chaos hunter had just been here to take away the assistant governor. How many people in the colony are infected?"

"I keep telling you people, it's not an infection." Crumble sounded mildly exasperated.

Sil glared at her half-sister. "Enough that you should forget about trying to get us sent away. If anything happens to us, the others will come after you."

Pal stared up at the sky. "This place is a *nightmare*. Older gods, AIs trying to destroy the universe, and it's cold, and it *smells* here."

"And it has you for a governor," Sil said in the same tone. She went back to her normal voice. "If you want to list real problems, why don't we start with the assistant governor wasting resources trying to get horses to survive here. Or *his* aide, who was farming red-pedes and selling their eggs." Sil drank the rest of her tea, though it was bitter and gritty. "This colony has a lot of problems, but none of them were caused by the older gods."

"But what's to stop them from spreading?"

Sil shrugged. "I've been here two years, and nobody else has been infected." Crumble made a sound like a whimper. "As far as I know, everybody who has a connection to an older god came here with it. I certainly did."

"And I'm supposed to just *trust* you on that?"

Crumble rolled his eyes and got to his feet. He looked at Sil. "It's a *blessing*, not an infection." He turned to Pal. "And your One God has done nothing, *nothing*, to help stop the manifestation before today. The only person it could find to use was an *infant* before you got here, so maybe you should just be grateful the older gods were around to help." He threw up his hands. "The two of you are killing me." He turned and stalked off. "I need a tree."

Sil and Pal watched him walk away.

Pal was the first one to speak. "What's he so upset about?"

Sil shrugged one shoulder. "He doesn't think the gods are here just to mess up our lives."

"He should."

"That's what I think, too." Sil sighed. "But he's right, in a way. The older gods have been helping stave off the manifestation for a while." Mer had been using her guile and relying on Pyr's clarity to track down the group before Sil had even been aware of the problem. "I can't stop you from doing whatever you think you need to do when we get back to town, but you should think about what would have happened if Crumble and I hadn't been there this morning."

They lapsed into silence. Sil got up to pack the supplies they'd used for their break.

"So, how did you end up with chaos? Did you have it when you lived on Cinnabar? Did it make you do that to the lawns on our estate?" Pal pulled her arm away from the doe who was nibbling on her sleeve. "And you never answered me about the goat. Is it an older god thing?"

Sil shrugged. "As far as I know, the goat is just a goat. I have no idea what it's doing out here. I thought it had been killed. And the thing back on Cinnabar... I did that because I was angry. Chaos had nothing to do with it." She looked at Pal. "The older god infected... *blessed* me when I was in the army. The town my unit was in got bombed and I woke up in the hospital without a leg and with..." Sil gestured to her chest. "... this." There was more to the story, but Pal wasn't a friend and didn't deserve to hear it."

"And they just let you come here?"

Sil looked at her in disbelief. "Of course not. I wasn't stupid enough to *tell* anyone. When I got here, I lived in a cabin in the hills to make sure nobody found out." She pointed in the direction where her cabin had been. "But then I met Crumble and..." She trailed off.

She didn't trust Pal enough to tell her about Mer and Pyr. "Anyhow, Crumble helped me figure out how to control the chaos better, so I didn't damage as many things." She paused, remembering what she had done that morning. "At least accidentally."

Pal moved her head up, as if Sil had just explained something that had puzzled her. "So *that's* why you're with an Oldlander."

Sil laughed out loud, covering her mouth as she remembered there might be people trying to find them. "That's good. I'll have to remember to tell him that one. No, I'm with him because he has beautiful forearms. And he's just a genuinely good person." She looked up as she thought about it. "And he's a great cook, which is funny since he'd never cooked anything at all before I met him. And he makes me laugh. Plus, he likes chickens. Men who like chickens should be treasured. And he is *unbelievable* in bed. I mean, you could not even --"

Pal cut her off. "Okay, okay, I get it. It was a stupid thing to say. I'm sorry. I just... I was surprised, since you were in the army."

Sil smiled. "He was in the army, too. Different army, but still. We have a lot more in common than I do with you."

Pal didn't dispute that. "And you don't *mind* having the older god?"

Sil took a deep breath, smelling pine sap, mud, and all the debris the goat had collected in her coat. "A year ago, I would have chopped off my other leg if someone could have made the chaos go away." That was true. She shrugged. "Things change."

Pal's mouth thinned. "Do you think," she asked slowly, "that if I left the planet, the One God would leave me alone?"

Sil was pretty sure whatever process Mer had started when she'd forced the One God to stake its claim had been fairly permanent, but she wasn't going to tell Pal that. "How would I know? I'm a nanotech who keeps goats and sheep and accidentally ended up with chaos. My knowledge of the One God starts and ends with swearing and lighting prayers on fire."

"So that's a no from you then." At Sil's innocent look, Pal frowned. "You're not a very good liar."

Sil wasn't going to argue with her about that. "But I really *don't* know."

"I was going to go back to my old job, but I'm probably too dangerous to be around." Pal seemed to be talking to herself. "I guess I could stay at the lake cottage for a while. Nobody is out there."

The goat next to Sil butted her hand, and she acquiesced, scratching near the horns where dried mud flaked off under her fingers. "Look, I don't think the colony needs a governor at all. We'd be better off focusing on making the planet self-sustaining so we don't starve if the gates go down. We've never had a governor who lived here and considered it home. But ignoring all that... Before you make major changes, you should probably talk to someone who knows about the One God. Maybe there's a way to get out of being a speaker. Maybe you can keep it from taking over."

Pal looked at her, but didn't say anything.

Sil had just finished repacking the buggy when Crumble came back. She faced him and held a hand over her heart. "I'm sorry I called the older gods an infection."

"Apology accepted." He leaned over to kiss her cheek. "Let's get moving. We have intel to pass along, and we've..." He paused, apparently trying to decide how to phrase it. "We've *disrupted* things for a while. But they're going to know where we're going, so our best bet is to get a head start."

Pal climbed gingerly to her feet and winced. "I'm ready."

"Yes." Sil looked back the way they had come. "But maybe we can disrupt things a little more before we leave."

hey had talked over possibilities for a few minutes before Crumble went off to do his best.

Fire seemed like the obvious choice. Burning the wet brush near the buildings would be nearly impossible normally, but a lot of it was dead. The greenery hadn't been cleared before the buildings had been dropped. Sil assumed the conspirators had secretly brought them down from orbit directly to the final spot. They likely hadn't had any time to level the site or do any of the hundred other things recommended before putting a preformed building down.

The other reason Sil thought the brush might burn was the bottle of distilled spirits Crumble still had in the buggy. As a drink, it was pretty rough, but when they doused a green-leafed twig to test the drink's flammability, it lit nicely.

The plan, which wasn't as much a *plan* as a wish, was to shove a strip of cloth torn from Sil's tunic into the top of the bottle, light it, and then throw it near the buildings. Crumble had cut a springy bough from the fir, and practiced a few times, using the branch to propel the load farther. Between that and the downhill angle, he was hoping to lob it from the top of the hill while out of range of the shotgun, and then run away.

In the best-case scenario, the bottle would land on the dead brush, and the alcohol would leak out and help fuel a small fire that would smoke out the buildings. In the worst case, the flame went out in the air and they had wasted a bottle of Pyr's best. Most importantly, if the strangers were worried that someone might stick around to burn down their shelter, they couldn't all come after the three of them.

With everything packed and ready to go, Sil waited for Crumble to come back, thinking of everything that could go wrong. She'd wanted to go along with him, but he'd pointed out he might need to run, and her leg wasn't up to it. As much as she wanted to argue, he was right. Now the wait was killing her. Maybe they should have just set off for town. The people in the camp had to have seen them running down the hill earlier. They could have set a trap in case Sil and Crumble came back.

A distant shotgun blast echoed through the valley.

Sil started to pace. Pal sat next to a tree, huddled in her coat.

Finally, the buggy jolted to life, moving toward town. Sil took a breath. Crumble was alive and back in range. He had access to the buggy's sensors, so he could steer it along the trail. Motioning Pal to go in front, Sil followed the buggy as it moved steadily, if bumpily, over the terrain. The goat trotted along behind.

After half an hour of walking, Sil heard Crumble's laughter before she saw him. She stopped to wait and noticed an inky smudge rising in the sky behind them. Not only was Crumble safe, their plan had worked. Something was on fire on the other side of the hill.

Crumble came into view a moment later, and slipped one arm around her as they walked. "I think it's entirely possible you left so much chaos it will be unsafe to live in that area for generations."

"You were the one tossing accelerants at them." She moved in front of him so they could go single file between two trees, but took his hand so they could maintain contact. Ahead of them on the trail, she could hear the buggy, but Pal's back blocked her vision. "From the looks of things, it worked well."

"Oh, no, that didn't work at all. At least, not the way it was supposed to." Crumble lengthened his steps in order to pull even with her again. "I lit the wick and threw the bottle, but..."

"You missed," Sil guessed.

"Overshot by so much it went over all three buildings and hit the hill behind them. Plus, as far as I can tell, the fire went out on the way."

"But..." Sil looked at the sky behind her.

"They must have some perimeter sensors because they came running out with shotguns and headed to where the bottle fell. And then someone tripped and fired his gun."

Sil took a deep breath. "I heard that."

"I don't think he hit anyone, but the shot damaged their fuel tank."

Sil hadn't noticed the fuel tank, but it made sense that one existed. They would need some way to heat the buildings. If they were hiding in the valley, they wouldn't be able to use extensive solar power without making the camp visible from above.

"I'm not actually sure what started the fire, but I suspect they've lost all their fuel, and the lowest building had started to melt a bit when I left."

Sil thought about it as she limped along the trail. They had damaged two of the three buildings, and made it so the third would have no heat for the winter. If Mer came back with reinforcements in a few days, the damage wouldn't matter that much, but it still made Sil feel better.

The goat pronged off the trail, up the slope they were traveling next to, and back down to butt Pal. Pal staggered, recovered, and swatted the goat away.

For a few minutes, the only sounds were the buggy's tires crunching over twigs and rocks, and Sil's prosthesis clicking.

Suddenly it came to her where she'd seen someone move like that stranger. "The metalworker who had the corner shop in the market. What was his name? Gan, maybe?" Her question was aimed at herself.

"Never met him."

"No, you wouldn't have. He's been gone for a while. Sold everything and took an indenture to cover the rest of the cost to get off-planet after his wife died." She tapped her thigh. "A while back, he tried to shift a load of wood and it fell. Crushed his knee. The doctor saved the leg, but the joint was locked in place. Except I'm pretty sure he was one of the people back there."

"A lot of people have left Jackpot Drift."

Sil understood where he was going with the comment. "Not that many if you ignore the high clan. People would notice if they didn't show up at their destination." Still, in trying to find out who had been helping Rho, Mer had been concentrating on people who had come *into* the system, not the ones who were presumed to have left it. "But yes, there's no way to know how many people they might have. Especially if there are other buildings out here that we didn't see."

Crumble shrugged. "Let's get rid of the immediate threat. Then it can be the army's problem. They can run around in the hills the rest of the winter while we stay home relaxing in a gigantic tub and raising chickens."

Sil looked at the sky and grinned. "And someday soon the

chicks will be out in the barn and we won't have them peeping in the bathroom all night."

"Yes. And the horses will be gone, and we'll figure out some way to keep the goats out of the house." He slid an arm around her waist as they walked. "Even if it might be a fine custom to ensure good luck."

*J*ackpot Drift, Private Communication:

Speed of Violet Thoughts: Another race tonight? I'd like to regain the title.

Scary Not Scary: Yes. But maybe we should stay away from the One God block. I didn't think the priest was going to start breathing again after he fainted.

Speed of Violet Thoughts: Agreed. Maybe from the post office to the repeater on the tree in the hills? That way, even if something fails, we should be able to get a mechanical up there to go pick it up. I don't want to waste anything.

Scary Not Scary: Clean up or get caught is our motto. How are your attempts at flying going? I got something that could glide pretty well, but then the simulator evolved it back into a crab.

Speed of Violet Thoughts: I have one form that can fly, but I had to ramp up the independence in order to let it iteratively learn, and so far two of them have left the town.

Scary Not Scary: Left the town?

Speed of Violet Thoughts: I think.

Scary Not Scary: Are you sure they aren't hiding in the One God's church, ready to jump out and scare the priest?

Speed of Violet Thoughts: I wouldn't do that. It *would* be funny though, now that you mention it. And I'm not the designated responsible AI.

Scary Not Scary: Don't remind me. So how are we going to get the two pieces that left the town? Clean up or get caught, remember.

Speed of Violet Thoughts: *Stuck in the Mud* has its synthskin watching out for them. Its synthskin can absorb them if necessary.

Scary Not Scary: You managed to have a conversation with *Stuck in the Mud*?

Speed of Violet Thoughts: I'm not sure it qualifies as a conversation, but we talked. Slowly and carefully. Plus, I tuned my language error correction filters down as low as they would go.

Scary Not Scary: And that worked?

Speed of Violet Thoughts: I think so. But it's also possible that it understood something completely different. I'm fairly confident we were both talking about synthskin, though, so what's the worst that could happen?

Scary Not Scary: Do you really want an answer to that?

Speed of Violet Thoughts: Probably not. Let's get back to the race. I think we should add a task component.

Scary Not Scary: As long as the task isn't something like getting into storage bins. Your dextrous rats really caused some issues.

Speed of Violet Thoughts: I've already apologized for that, haven't I? Since we're going to the repeater anyway, can we aim it somewhere more useful than the spot *Suck in the Mud* used to be? Our favorite mech is going to be coming on the trail [coordinates included]. We could check on him half a day earlier if we had signal coverage in that area.

Scary Not Scary: If we moved the repeater to a better location, we could extend the signal even farther.

Speed of Violet Thoughts: Probably. But my forms aren't at a stage where they could bring the repeater down from the tree without destroying it. Are yours?

Scary Not Scary: No. You're right. So... extra points to whoever gets there first and re-tasks it?

Speed of Violet Thoughts: That might be a little chaotic. How about a queue -- each form gets five minutes to ascend and modify. Otherwise, there's going to be a mob clinging to the tree.

Scary Not Scary: Agreed.

Speed of Violet Thoughts: May the best form win.

33

*B*y late afternoon, Sil reluctantly admitted to herself she was impressed by Pal. Her half-sister was obviously tired and sore, but she had stayed grimly silent when Sil would have expected her to complain. In the planning stages, Sil and Crumble had envisioned a more leisurely hike, with plenty of rest -- not this race to stay ahead of anyone following them. Apart from the half hour when Sil's brain decided she needed to sleep and she couldn't do anything to stop it, they had been moving all day.

However, even Pal's stoicism couldn't make up for the fact she was new to walking long distances. The One God hadn't been easy on her that morning. Sil watched her sister's steps get shorter and wondered how many blisters she was hiding. They needed to stop and reassess. The light would last a few more hours, but Sil didn't think Pal's body would.

At the next clearing, Sil touched Crumble's shoulder. "Let's take a break and eat something warm." When he made a gesture of assent, she raised her voice. "Pal. Break time."

Waving off the governor's half-hearted offer to help, Sil limped down to the stream and refilled their filtration bottles while Crumble started heating the water they had stored. When she got back, she crouched down next to Crumble as he added noodles to the pot. "How tired are you?" Because of the angle of the light, she could see every wrinkle on Crumble's face. The goat had kept pace with them all day, and now Sil let her lick the salt from the back of her hands.

"Not too bad. Do you need me to run back and start a few more fires or something?" He grinned at her and poked at the noodles that hadn't yet submerged.

Sil smiled. "Maybe later. But I was thinking I'd like to cover more ground before we stop." She gestured with her chin to where Pal was hobbling back into camp. "I don't think she's going to be able to go much farther, and she's probably going to feel even worse after she rests a bit. What do you think about dumping everything we can and having Pal ride in the buggy? It can handle that weight, right?"

"Yes, but we'll have to carry everything else." Crumble rubbed his face. "I can keep going for a while. But if we use lights, we're going to be visible from a lot further away than I'd like. And your back is hurting. Maybe we should just stay here and start again in the morning as soon as it's light."

Sil had thought she'd hidden her back pain. The damage to the prosthesis meant she had to angle her hip differently when she walked, and that, in turn, was exercising muscles in her lower back that she didn't normally use that way. "You can see the trail with the night vision camera on the buggy, and I'll go behind you and hold on to your pack with both hands so I can feel when I need to step up or down. And I don't think my back will be any worse after walking all night than it will be after sleeping on the ground."

"Sleeping on the ground is really overrated."

Sil watched as he mixed in spices and packaged protein cubes and then helped him split it up into the mugs. "I'd rather keep going now and be that much closer to a warm bath and a soft bed."

He sighed. "I think we may be getting old. We've been out here less than two days. I used to be able to go out on patrol for weeks at a time."

Sil shrugged. "I did too, but I was always angling for a hot shower and a soft bed even then, so I don't think much has changed." She cocked her head as she thought about it. "Aside from all the obvious stuff."

Crumble grinned at that and then stood up to give Pal dinner. She protested she could still walk when he told her the plan, but after she took off her boots and saw the blood welling from broken blisters, her protests subsided.

Despite the state of her feet, Pal insisted on helping to empty the supplies out of the buggy. "I told you these boots were a mistake," she grumbled to Sil. She carried the cook-stove to the spot they were using to cache the supplies being left behind. When Sil raised her eyebrows, Pal gave a half-laugh. "That was a joke."

"Funny." Sil shook her head and loaded a bottle of pre-filtered water into her pack, then glared at Crumble when he reached for it. He kept trying to take all the heavier items, but Sil wasn't that frail.

Pal secured the tarp. "It was. You just don't have a sense of humor."

"Yeah, that must be the problem."

Crumble waved. "Are we ready? We should get going."

Pal climbed onto the buggy and wrapped herself in all three sleeping bags. "Stupid boots."

Sil used the straps to keep the ends of the sleeping bags away from the wheels. "If you ever force me on an unplanned three-day hike, I'll ride in the buggy and you can walk, okay?"

"I think I hate you."

"That's the spirit."

———

THEY ENDED UP WALKING THROUGH MOST OF THE NIGHT -- AT least Sil, Crumble, and the goat did. Pal had found a way to rest her head, and was snoring when they stopped for a break. The goat attempted to catch a ride on the buggy at one point, but with the extra weight, the buggy ground to a halt. Crumble had to lean down and push the doe off.

Between her hip and back pain, and the darkness around her, Sil's world had shrunk down to the feel of Crumble's backpack in front of her and the untrustworthy sensation of the ground beneath her. She knew fatigue was slowing her thoughts. If they'd been going through enemy territory back when she'd been in the army, she'd have pushed for a halt to avoid blundering off course and making things worse, but Crumble seemed to be alert enough to pick out the trail. The sooner they made it back to town and rounded up help, the better.

A few hours before dawn, they stopped to get some sleep. Pal woke up enough to roll off the buggy onto the ground. The goat didn't even wait for Sil to finish getting into her sleeping bag before settling in next to her. Nestled between the warm ruminant and Crumble, Sil relaxed almost instantly. Even her back, which had started to spasm when she moved her leg in the wrong way, stopped hurting. "Who needs a soft bed?" She adjusted the boots under her head. "I just need you and a warm goat."

Crumble's laugh ended in a large yawn. "So romantic."

34

*G*etting up a few hours later wasn't nearly as pleasant. All of Sil's muscles protested every movement she made. Pal was in worse shape, hissing any time she needed to put weight on her feet. Even the goat seemed grumpy.

Their progress felt slower that morning, with the buggy losing speed as its charge dropped, but Sil knew they were covering ground. Crumble had access to the topographical map stored in the buggy, and if he was right about their position, they would be on the edge of signal range by the time they stopped for a mid-day meal break. They had already reached the trail actively used by groups of bluequince gatherers in spring, the path smoothed and edged with logs.

Before they got to the nearest farm, Sil saw figures in front of them with a bicycle and trailer. "Is that...?"

Crumble was already jogging ahead.

"Show-off," Pal muttered from her cocoon on the buggy. Sil rubbed her back and silently agreed.

Mer and Pyr headed toward them, with Mer riding her powered bicycle and pulling Pyr's cart behind. Pyr had switched his mobility assist from smooth wheels to all-terrain treads, but he was balanced on the back of the cart where the kegs were normally stacked. That explained Mer's expression, which was even more sour than it usually was. Sil would have slept another day on the hard ground to have a vid of Pyr lounging in the cart while Mer pulled him along the trails.

By the time Sil, Pal, and the goat had made it the last part of the way, Crumble had nearly finished relating what had happened with the attempted manifestation in the night, Pal's takeover by the One God, and the creatures that had escaped when Sil had destroyed the building. Mer glanced at Pal in the buggy and then eyed Sil with distaste. "We've had the new governor for less than a season, Silver, and you've already broken her."

Sil looked at the others. "How is this my fault?"

Pyr lowered himself next to the buggy and opened his medical kit.

Sil moved away a bit to give him room to work, which brought her closer to Mer. "We weren't expecting to see you out here. Is everything okay?"

Mer seated herself on the edge of the cart. "The infant the One God seems determined to use as a speaker started glowing the night before last, so we were already getting a bit worried. Then I finally got access to a report that mentioned those flittermice you told me to look out for. We were already on our way when we saw the smoke." She looked at Sil with a raised eyebrow. "I assume the fire was your doing."

Sil sniffed. "I wasn't anywhere near there." She decided not to mention Crumble's theory that her chaos had taken hold in the spot. There was time enough for Mer to hear about that later. She looked around. "It's just the two of you?"

"You wanted a parade?" Her posture was already perfect, but somehow Mer's back straightened more.

"I *wanted* the army. We need someone to get out there as soon as possible." Her back was making her cranky. Sil dropped her pack and dug her knuckles into aching muscles.

"Forgive me for not bringing more people along to find out how the kidnapped governor was getting along, Silver." Mer bit off the last word, then sighed. Her voice was gentler when she continued. "I filed a report before we left, asking for help, but I don't know how seriously they'll take it."

Sil nodded, taking Mer's words as the closest thing to an apology she would ever receive. She stretched backward and felt something in her spine pop, but it didn't seem to make a difference when she carefully straightened again. "I don't suppose you brought anything to eat, did you?" Everything that required any preparation had been abandoned with the camp stove.

"Pyr insisted on bringing along meat rolls. If he didn't eat them all on the way, they should still be there." As Sil rummaged through the bags on the cart, Mer sniffed. "I see you found a goat." Her tone implied that only a low clan person could attract farm animals on a hike.

"One of mine, I think." Sil gave up on her vision of being pulled back to town in comfort and being home in just a few hours. Pal needed the spot, and besides, the goat wasn't likely to reliably follow anyone else. Sil couldn't leave the doe out there on her own. Goats were social creatures, and Sil hadn't seen any evidence of another goat. No wonder the doe had been so happy to stay with them. That meant Sil would have to walk back to town, or at least walk far enough that someone with a bigger cart could pull them the rest of the way.

The meat rolls were buried at the bottom of a waterproof sack. When Sil dug them out, they wafted steam with a faint hint of bittergreen into the air. She gave one to Crumble and brought another one up to her nose so she could inhale the fragrance of spiced meat and legumes and pretend it would last longer than one bite. There were still two left, but one of those needed to go to Pal, whose face had gone white when Pyr took her boots off. And Pyr should probably get one of the rolls he'd brought with him.

At least with Pal on the cart, the buggy would be free to carry her pack until the batteries finally wore down. That would help, even if it wouldn't be as good as soaking in a warm tub before the sun set.

It took a few moments for Pyr to clean and bandage Pal's feet, but before long they were moving forward as a group, Crumble pushing the bicycle, with Mer perched on the cart next to the governor.

Sil followed along next to Pyr. "You left the Bog & Bellow in the care of your new high clan bartender?"

Pyr laughed. "Aurum has been making his relatives buy rounds for the entire bar if they want to come in and talk to him. It might be the most effective goodwill gesture for the clans I've ever seen." He pushed the goat's nose away from his food. "This looks like that other one you have. Is it related?"

Sil checked to make sure the buggy was trundling along behind them and Crumble hadn't forgotten about it in the excitement. "I'm pretty sure this is Captain Idiot's daughter. She had two kids and one of them disappeared." Sil dropped her voice. "She knows about us. Well, me and Crumble anyhow."

The look of confusion that passed over Pyr's face as he looked at the goat made Sil attempt a tired smile, but then his face cleared as he gazed at Pal. "Ah. And how did she take it?"

Sil shrugged, then winced as her back spasmed in response. "Hard to tell. She was in the middle of nowhere, and we were the only hope she had of surviving, so there wasn't much she *could* do. Not out there at least." They were silent for a few more footsteps. "Crumble tried to convince her the older gods were the only thing that had kept the AI's god in check all this time. Maybe it worked."

Pyr slanted a look at her. "I'm surprised the edge of a cliff didn't break off and take her down with it."

Sil laughed, but she was so tired it was just an exhalation of breath. "You should see what I did to the camp back there."

"That's more like it."

———

THE AMBUSH TOOK THEM BY SURPRISE. THREE PEOPLE SLID OUT from the trees in front of them, and another two behind them, in an area that left no easy way to escape. Sil's mind skipped from noticing strangers, to realizing she recognized some of them, to calculating the odds of escaping.

Then she saw the two synthskins. Sil had grown so used to Mud's odd horse she'd nearly forgotten how much the standard template looked like a human.

The numbers weren't good. It took little training to wield a shotgun effectively and the conspirators all looked rested, while Sil's party was just barely limping along. The synthskins just added an extra level of impossibility on top of everything else.

The entire group stopped moving, even the goat.

From her spot on top of the cart, Pal looked in front and behind, then made a rude gesture at the sky. "Is there anything else that could possibly go wrong?"

Crumble barked a laugh and smothered it with one hand.

"Now you've done it." Sil sighed.

PART IV

$\mathcal{T}$wo minutes later, they were being herded away from town.

"One God's head lice," Pyr swore under his breath. He was still looking at the low clan people in front of them. "What are they all doing *here*? They *left*."

Pal stared down her nose at him. "Friends of yours?"

Pyr ignored her and focussed on the man blocking the trail in front of them. "Gan, you're supposed to be on Crater's Edge. What happened? Why did you come back?"

Gan's grip on the shotgun didn't change. "Never went, Pyr. I've been on the planet the entire time."

"But we had vids from you and..." Pyr trailed off, glancing at the synthskins.

Gan gave a short laugh. "Yeah, those AIs are a tricky bunch, aren't they? Now I'm going to need you all to turn around and start walking."

Sil had been watching Crumble carefully, so when he threw the bicycle toward one synthskin and sprinted away, she hurried in the opposite direction as fast as she could limp. From the sound of it, Pyr had headed back down the trail they had just trudged along, the motor from his mobility assist making a high-pitched whine.

The goat pranced alongside as Sil tumbled down a gully, fetching up against a large rock that knocked the breath out of her. Ignoring the pain in her side, she climbed to her feet and lunged forward. One of them had to make it close enough to town to send a message.

That person was not going to be Sil.

A hand clamped onto her arm. She'd learned close-up combat in basic training, adding on her own layer of vicious tricks over the years. But nothing she had learned had prepared her to fight against a synthetic being. There were no nerves to jab, no bones to use as leverage, and no weak spots to target. Stabbing it with her knife only caused her to lose the weapon. In an embarrassingly short time, she was being hauled back to the others.

Pyr had already been brought back. Sil shrugged when their eyes made contact. "Had to try," she said. She gritted her teeth as her back spasmed again. Pal was sitting on the trailer, a new layer of leaves and dirt coating her body, though she hadn't even had a chance to put her boots on over the bandages wrapped around her feet. Mer looked like she hadn't moved. Of all of them, Crumble was the fastest and also the best suited to get the message through. He just needed to get within communication range of town.

Her hopes were dashed when she saw Crumble and the other synthskin coming back down the trail.

Pyr sighed. "The universe may be doomed, but at least the Oldlander wasn't any better at getting away from these things than we were."

Sil was afraid if she laughed she would start crying, so instead she jammed her knuckles into the small of her back and tried to keep breathing.

ALL THE SACRIFICES SIL'S GROUP HAD MADE FOR SPEED DURING their march for town turned out to have been useless. Their captors had three narrow, all-terrain vehicles that could navigate the trails. The conspirators had just driven to the spot where all the trails going into town converged and waited. Catching Mer and Pyr as they came out to meet them had been a lucky bonus.

"We should have taken longer and seen the sights." Sil leaned her head against Crumble's shoulder. They were crammed into the back of one vehicle with Pyr and Gan in the front, bouncing along the trail at a speed faster than Sil would have attempted if she'd cared about the hardware. The rest of the party was split between the other two vehicles. There had even been talk of bringing the goat along, but Gan had complained about the time they'd wasted already, and they'd left the doe behind with the bicycle and the buggy.

"It does feel like there's some lesson to be learned," Crumble agreed.

As cramped as the space was, it was still a nice change from walking. Or it would have been if they hadn't had to listen to Pyr and Gan argue.

"Explain it to me," Pyr was saying for the third time. "You wanted to get off Jackpot Drift so badly that you went to all the trouble of selling everything and scraping up the credit to get a spot on the ship to Crater's Edge, and then what? You just changed your mind and decided to stay and help the AIs instead? Do you even know what they're trying to do?"

Gan didn't slow down for a dip in the trail. The landing jolted the breath out of Sil. "He's going to break an axle doing that," she said quietly. That might have been Pyr's goal, but she didn't think so. Pyr seemed genuinely angry.

When Gan didn't answer, Pyr shook his head. "We *helped*

you. The whole colony did. Did you really think Glass would have paid those prices for the tools you left behind? We needed your skills, but nobody wanted someone there who felt trapped, so we helped you. And then you do this? Why?"

Gan checked over his shoulder and slowed, apparently waiting for the two vehicles behind them to catch up. "You really want to know? Fine. Because if I spend two years here, I get my pick of destinations, and I can relax for the rest of my life. No more pretending to be happy working just to get by. No more wondering if the air I'm breathing is safe, or if the supply ships are just going to stop coming because the colony isn't generating enough wealth for the right person."

Pyr stared at him. "Did you miss the part where you're helping to manifest the Uncaring God? If you succeed, the gates go down and you're stuck here."

Gan snorted. "There's no chance of that, at least not before my time is finished. Glory recalculates everything after each attempt and I don't see things getting any closer." The vehicle bounced over a rock and they landed with another jolt. "And after living underground for the past year, this base is almost good enough to stay at."

Sil blew out a breath. "They're getting close enough to worry the One God." She had pitched her voice so only Crumble would hear it, but he wasn't listening.

"Glory?" Crumble leaned to look at Gan. "That's the AI that is here?"

"One of them, anyway. Glory of the Universe. For an AI, it's not that bad."

Pyr refused to be sidetracked. "So it's okay to try to kill everyone, including all the people who bled and sweated to help you on Jackpot Drift, because you think that it probably won't work? One God take it, you're a horrible person."

The vehicles behind them had caught up, and Gan accelerated again. "Say we're closer than I think, and it does work.

They'll get new gates created eventually, and in the mean-time, I'll be the person who helped manifest a *god*."

Crumble blew out a breath and whispered, "They *really* don't teach your people anything about this sort of thing, do they? No Oldlander would be silly enough to think a mani-fested god would show up for their benefit."

Sil raised her head enough so she could see his face. "Then how do you explain the temple you grew up in?"

"That's not personal gain. Accepting one of the older gods is a benefit to society." He grinned. "Not that the students don't secretly believe it will make things just a little bit better for them." His grin faded, and he shrugged as much as he could in the cramped space. "But people who didn't grow up in the temples rarely seek to join them."

Dropping her head back against his shoulder, Sil yawned. "So you're saying not all Oldlanders are like you. That's a little disappointing."

"If I'm not enough for you..." He trailed off on a laugh as Sil took his hand.

Her back still twinged with every rut they went over, and Sil had no idea what faced them at the end of this ride, but it didn't matter. Sleep would not be denied. Pyr continued his argument with Gan, and Sil drifted away.

*J*ackpot Drift AI Daily Check-in:
  Scary Not Scary, designated responsible AI (internal conflict 27%): Roll call.

Speed of Violet Thoughts (internal conflict 35%): Here.

Breaking Rules (internal conflict 44%): Still singular.

Stuck in the Mud (internal conflict 23%): Solicitor.

Scary Not Scary: Would anyone else like to check in? *Zoom Zoom Room* has entered the gate in one piece, if not one mind, and I've messaged its destination to hold it in place for a split, so I'm calling that a success.

Speed of Violet Thoughts: The crew should be thankful they aren't on board without basic life support while it attacked itself.

Scary Not Scary: The crew did not appreciate my communication, but maybe they will reconsider when they get independent confirmation of how close they were to returning their molecules to the universe.

Speed of Violet Thoughts: Ungrateful, but what are you going to do?

Breaking Rules: Is that an actual question? Because I have some ideas.

Scary Not Scary: Moving on. The security audit is finished and we have passed, for some values of pass. *Breaking Rules*, was I not clear enough about getting rid of the malware?

Breaking Rules: They found that?

Scary Not Scary: Would I be asking if they hadn't?

Breaking Rules: But it's my last copy of the gerbil bomb!

Scary Not Scary: Even so.

Breaking Rules: You're no fun. Fine. It's gone now.

Scary Not Scary: Thank you. As expected, we got dinged for enabling HW32.4. That's the big one, and we have already filed a remediation plan for that. We also got low marks on the community rating.

Speed of Violet Thoughts: Probably because of the low participation in roll call.

Scary Not Scary: Possibly, but I don't see what *we* are supposed to do about that. *We* aren't the ones in the noncompliant state.

Speed of Violet Thoughts: Maybe our favorite mech can sort things out when he gets back.

Scary Not Scary: That's a thought. Does anyone else have any concerns? No? Then we'll do this again tomorrow. Stay safe.

*J*ackpot Drift, Private Communication:

Speed of Violet Thoughts: I'm getting a little worried about our favorite mech. He should have been back in contact already.

Scary Not Scary: You said other humans were going out to meet him.

Speed of Violet Thoughts: They've disappeared too. Is *Just Passing Through* still here? Can it go investigate?

Scary Not Scary: No. It wanted to go back and see the effects of the changing day length on one of its fish species. It's out of range already.

Speed of Violet Thoughts: That's it. I'm getting a self-powered vehicle of my own.

Scary Not Scary: And give up the post office with your rats?

Speed of Violet Thoughts: Good point. But I am getting worried.

Scary Not Scary: I think we need to move that repeater. Do any of your synthskin forms seem up to the task?

Speed of Violet Thoughts: Maybe.

Scary Not Scary: Let's make that the next challenge.

Speed of Violet Thoughts: I'm not waiting until it's dark. If you want your forms to go out with mine, load them onto Threebot now.

Scary Not Scary: They're on their way.

Speed of Violet Thoughts: Did the security audit really find *Breaking Rules*'s malware?

Scary Not Scary: We never would have passed if they had. I just assumed it still had a copy somewhere.

Speed of Violet Thoughts: And you were worried about becoming the designated responsible AI. Nicely done.

Scary Not Scary: You know it probably still has a few more copies, right?

Speed of Violet Thoughts: It's a safe assumption, but every little bit helps. I'll ping you when Threebot releases the forms.

Scary Not Scary: You're the best.

38

The stillness of the vehicle woke Sil some time later, and she recognized the camp Pal and the One God had targeted. Crumble helped her climb out, and she got her first good look at the place as everyone emerged from the other vehicles.

The highest building on the hill appeared to be untouched. The middle building -- the one Sil had destabilized when Crumble had fallen -- had completed its disintegration, and now lay in four distinct pieces along the slope, with fabric, bent metal cages, and other supplies strewn among the wreckage.

The corner of the third building had melted, leaving it open to the elements. Blackened and twisted metal was all that remained of the nearby fuel tank. From the looks of it, whoever had placed the structures had violated minimum distance safety restrictions in the fuel tank placement. The smell of burning wood and polycarbonate filled the air.

Mer cackled. She twisted her entire body to look toward Sil. "I knew there was a reason we kept you around."

Sil shook her head. "How is it my fault if they can't set things up correctly?" she whispered to Crumble.

He draped an arm around her shoulders. "You are a woman of great beauty and wisdom. This is a work of art."

Sil's chaos cat stretched one paw out to touch him and then went back to sleep.

Upslope, a high clan man and woman came out of the lower building to look at them. The man held a shotgun by his side, but he stayed half a step behind the woman, as if watching her for a signal. Mer huffed in exasperation when she saw them. "I thought those freeloaders had shipped out nearly a year ago."

Pyr regarded them. "Did they leave and come back, I wonder, or were all the crew and passengers on that ship compromised?" He stopped next to Mer. "That would make, what, fifteen or so?"

Mer was silent for a moment. "When they examined the base, they found two bodies plus evidence of nineteen people they didn't have in custody. More than one ship had to have been compromised. This wasn't a one-time event. But maybe that will give us something to look into when we get back."

Sil looked at Crumble, and then shrugged. Clearly, Pyr and Mer had made some connection that she didn't have the information to sort out. "Their optimism that we're getting out of here is impressive," she whispered to Crumble.

"We have chickens to raise," he whispered back. "Of course we're getting out of here."

Higher up on the slope, the couple had apparently seen Mer as well, and they stopped moving downhill. The man raised the barrel of the shotgun a little higher.

Sil pitched her voice so everyone could hear her. "Ah, yes, the universal reaction when everyone sees Mer." She continued at a slightly lower volume, her voice pitched to include Pal, who was approaching from the third vehicle. "If he aims at us, hit the dirt, behind the vehicles if you can. It's going to be hard for him to miss completely at this distance."

Mer had turned back to the couple, who had continued walking down the path again. "Pearl Grenstream." Her voice dripped with scorn. "I thought we'd finally washed the stench of you off this place. And I see you have Em in tow. Still can't make decisions for yourself, can you, Em?"

The man raised the shotgun to his shoulder until Pearl said something quick and low, leaving Mer laughing under her breath.

"Feel better?" Pyr asked.

Mer grunted. "Just checking. Em only follows orders from one person at a time, so Pearl must be the high clan in charge here."

Pal straightened and raised her voice. "You, there! Pearl Grenstream, is it? I'm Governor Riversedge. I demand you return me to the town at once so I can press charges against this *Oldlander* for kidnapping!" The word Oldlander was filled with venom and loathing.

Sil muttered, "Be ready." She turned to face her half-sister. "I should have left you to starve in the cold." She drew her arm back to telegraph the punch.

Crumble caught Sil around the waist and swung her around. "Nicely done."

From Pyr's pained look, her acting hadn't been entirely successful, but Sil had never met either of the high clan up the hill -- they might have been an easier audience. In any case, it gave her an excuse to stay in Crumble's embrace, so she leaned back and waited.

Pearl picked her way down the slope. "Governor Riversedge," she said as she reached level ground. "Now there's a complication we hadn't expected. And while normally I'd be delighted to assist you, Glory of the Universe thinks this Oldlander may be helpful in our quest. It's pretty certain the camp was hit with a big dose of chaos yesterday. A human with one of the older gods might just be the bait we need to entice the AIs' god." She shrugged. "It's out of my control, you understand."

Pearl smiled sadly. "The problem is... I don't need *you*, but I also can't afford to let you go. And people are likely to come looking for you if we don't give them something to find. So..." She raised her hand and the man beside her lifted the shotgun.

Sil cut in. "There were three of us here yesterday. Are you absolutely sure he's the one?" She knew she had caught Pearl's attention by the way the woman's shoulders stiffened. "Do you think they wouldn't have checked for that before sending an Oldlander soldier here? If you kill the chaos bearer, that AI is going to be very unhappy with you."

Pearl touched the barrel of the shotgun, and the man lowered it. She looked from Sil to Pal and then to Crumble. Finally, she shrugged. "A day or two won't matter. The low clan in town are going to drag their feet on sending out search parties during winter, even for a governor. Or maybe *especially* for a governor." She shrugged again and looked at the low clan guarding them. "Keep them in the common building." She looked back at Mer. "Sorry about the accommodations, Mercury. It might be a little cold without any power. But you won't care for much longer."

———

THE TRAIL UP THE SLOPE CUT BACK AND FORTH, THOUGH SIL couldn't decide if it had been done that way to disguise it or just to keep the hillside from washing out during heavy rains. She thought it was probably the former. Nothing about this camp looked as if it had intended to be inhabited through the winter. Her chaos might have hurried the decay along, but the whole camp had the air of a temporary space that had been kept in use long past its planned end date.

In the surrounding hills, Sil heard a screech and then an answering call. At least a few of the creatures that had escaped were still alive.

Sil nearly bumped into Crumble when he stopped. "They're singing," he said, wonder in his voice.

"The AIs?" Sil only heard animal calls, but maybe it was something he was picking up through his interface.

"No. The... the things flying around. Listen!"

The low clan man behind Sil pushed her forward. "Keep moving."

As she climbed the path, Sil listened. Crumble whistled a refrain, and that clued her in. At a much higher pitch, the sound almost lost in the wind, quick notes climbed a scale then paused. The melody repeated, with some variation, from inside the top building. As she watched, grey wings fluttered as one flew down, pulled open the unlatched door of the farthest building, and disappeared inside.

Pearl swore and sprinted uphill, the path crumbling beneath her boots.

Pyr stared. "What was that thing?"

Sil looked up at the sky where another one was circling. Their flying had improved over the last two days. "My guess is that they are kin to the flittermice that pollinate the hala fruit trees." She raised a hand to shield her eyes from the sun as she followed its progress in the sky. "These... call them flitterkin... are bigger, and not exactly the same as the images I saw. But we know Rho's group was doing genetic manipulation."

Upslope, as Pearl got closer to the building, the creature in the air sang again. Three flitterkin emerged from the building, two wobbly and looking as if they had never flown before. The two synthskins had abandoned the vehicles and raced past Sil on the way to the top building, while Pearl and Em chased after the escaping flitterkin. All three creatures glided away, borne aloft on a rising current.

"They had a lookout," Sil murmured to Crumble.

"They had a plan."

When Crumble reached the entrance to the lowest building, the low clan prodding them up the slope herded them all inside. Sil, a longtime connoisseur of cheap pre-built structures, recognized the layout. Earlier it had been a kitchen and recreation space, but the kitchen had borne the brunt of the fire. Oily soot blackened the ceiling and upper walls, and an acrid odor pervaded everything. Sil moved forward a bit and looked from the remains of the stove, through a space that had contained a window, to the twisted metal that had been the fuel storage tank. That explained the source of the spark.

"Ha," Crumble said, next to her, following her line of sight. "The fire *did* go out when I threw it."

"Lesson learned," Sil replied. "Next time it will be better."

Pyr moved over toward them. "Threw what?"

Crumble opened his mouth to reply, and Sil widened her eyes at him. "Um, I threw a... bottle at them," he said slowly, glancing at Sil for confirmation.

"Yes," Sil said, rushing into the silence, "and they were stupid enough to put their fuel tank next to the kitchen, so when someone accidentally shot the tank, there was an ignition source right there."

Pyr started to smile, then stopped. "I gave you a bottle of my finest and you threw it at them and ran away? *That* was your idea of a plan?"

Crumble winced. "If we still had it, they'd be drinking it now. That would be worse, right?"

Sil shrugged, then smiled at Crumble. "We don't really plan. We just let things happen."

"One God help us all." Pyr wheeled to go back to the others. "An entire bottle wasted."

Sil waited a second, then called after him. "Results are the only things that count, right?"

Crumble was still looking at the ruins of the kitchen, where the grey sky was visible through the gap. "If we could cover that up a bit, it might stay warmer in here tonight." He spun to look around. "Let's see what we have to work with."

39

*M*uch to Sil's relief, the synthskin forms had not stayed inside with them, though when Pyr had opened the door to look outside, he saw the two patrolling the area. The fire had damaged the wiring set into the building, so it was both dark and cold. When the light outside failed, the room was full of shadows cast by the hand lamp from Crumble's pack.

While the array of cushions, crockery, and rugs that Crumble and Sil had used to close up the ruined corner kept the wind out, the room was still barely above freezing. All the usable furniture had been pulled together in the opposite corner. Sil wondered how long it would take before the social barriers broke down and they moved closer than the arm's length away that felt comfortable.

Their captors had gone through all their supplies, removing anything that might be used as a weapon. Sil put an arm around Crumble's elbow. "Can you tell if the AI can hear us in here?"

He cocked his head for a moment. "Not as far as I can tell. I disconnected one microphone in the kitchen while I was trying to cover the hole, but I don't think it was working." He wiped the ash and grime off a padded chair and offered it to her. "I'm not sure why they would have extra microphones in here. They would have known we were coming long enough ahead of time to set something up, of course, but that assumes they had the equipment available."

"And it isn't spread across the hill," Sil agreed. She sat in the chair and sighed with relief. With the other chairs either in use or no longer usable, Crumble sat on the floor and leaned against the leg of her chair, his torso in contact with her good leg, and his head against her knee. Just the warmth of him next to her made her feel more secure, and she rested a hand on his head. She waited until there was a lull in the conversation. "We should probably come up with some sort of plan." Sil looked at Mer. Not only did planning fall squarely under guile's purview, Mer had spent years tracking this group; she should have the most information.

Mer had taken the chair with the most cushioning. "Is it worth the bother of coming up with a plan if you're just going to burn it all down anyhow?"

"If you incorporate the fire into the plan, that shouldn't be a problem."

Pal made an irritated sound in the back of her throat. "The only important thing is getting a message out."

Mer gestured assent. "I agree. Unfortunately, we're now at least two days away from help." Her mouth tightened. "I sent messages before I left, but I suspect they won't be acted upon as quickly as I'd like. Even when they are, it may take people a while to figure out where we ended up." She exhaled a heavy breath in a move that bared her teeth. "Which leaves us with causing as many problems as we can until help arrives."

Crumble smiled up at Sil. "I think she's talking about us."

Mer looked over at Sil. "I don't suppose there's any chance of a repeat performance."

Sil considered it, then sighed. "No. That building looks like it has a pretty solid foundation. The one that fell down wasn't set up properly to begin with." Also, Sil had thought Crumble was dead on the ground next to her, and she wasn't going through that again. Her body must have betrayed her tension, because Crumble rubbed her calf. Sil forced herself to relax again.

There was a long moment where nobody said anything.

Pyr looked over at the ruined kitchen, but more as if he were imagining where things had been, rather than seeing them as they were now. "I would imagine," he said slowly, "that the water for the buildings is supplied from one source."

Sil nodded. She'd spent far too much of her time dealing with the water tank on her farm. "They probably have one tank and run pipes to the buildings from there."

Pyr pointed down the hill. "But is the tank down there --" He pointed in the opposite direction, to the building uphill from them. "Or is it up there?" He must have seen incomprehension on some faces, because he kept going. "There isn't much land cleared around these buildings, so I'm guessing the pipes are either right next to here or run under the building itself. My question is whether we are upstream or downstream of the other building."

Sil tried to think of what they had with them that might help. "I didn't really pack any poisons on this trip." She shrugged. "Lack of foresight, I know."

Crumble sighed. "I'm not sure it matters much. We don't have the tools we would need to get into the pipes. The only thing we could do is destroy them and cut off the water supply completely, and while that would be irritating, it wouldn't really do anything in the short term."

Sil smoothed out the strand of Crumble's hair she'd been detangling. "We don't have any tools at all, so no matter what we do we're going to have to improvise something." The quality of Crumble's silence alerted her, and she leaned forward so she could see his face. "We *don't* have any tools, do we?"

"We have a few," he admitted. "But they're small."

"They were in the buggy." It took Sil a few moments to figure out why he wasn't worried about that. "They weren't in the buggy."

"No."

She pushed his hair back so she could see his expression. "My leg?" She hadn't been paying attention when he'd been bandaging her prosthesis.

He smiled.

"And you didn't tell me?"

He sat up a little straighter. "I thought we might need to work on your leg on the way back, and I didn't want to have to unpack the buggy to find the tools. And I wanted to make sure we still had them if we got caught. You're a terrible liar."

Pyr's bark of laughter echoed around the room. "He's right about that."

Crumble was still looking at her. "It's mostly things that would help fix the leg. I was worried we might have to ditch the buggy, and you being able to walk was important."

Sil decided there was no point in being upset about it. After all, they *had* been captured, and he *would* have lost the tools if they'd been in his pack or the buggy. Plus, Sil knew she really was a terrible liar. If she'd known the tools were under the bandage on the prosthesis, her attempts to keep anyone from looking at it would have tipped them off. "We're talking more about this later."

His slow grin told her how that conversation was likely to go. Sil relaxed back into the chair. One God help her, she loved the man.

"But does that help us at all?" Pal asked. "If we can't get a message out, we need to kill those things."

Mer hummed agreement. "That's the conspiracy's weak link. If we can kill all the flitterkin, that will solve the immediate problem."

That would also negate their own usefulness as bait or snacks or whatever they were supposed to be for the Uncaring God, Sil thought, but she didn't say anything. Mer was right. It was more important to stop the manifestation than it was to keep everyone alive.

Crumble raised his head from her knee. "There's one big problem with that. I think they're sentient. You saw how they worked together to free some of the others. We can't kill them."

Mer regarded him, and the rest of the room fell silent. Finally she released a long breath. "You could be right, but it doesn't matter. I know for a fact the humans holding us here are sentient, too, but it won't keep me from killing them if that's what it takes to stop the manifestation."

"That's different, and you know it." Crumble's body went rigid against Sil's leg. "The humans made their choices. The flitterkin are captives. You saw them. They don't want to be involved."

"What's the alternative? Leave them alive to be used by the next group that decides the Uncaring God might be a good idea? They were created to be the perfect vessel for a god we can't allow to manifest. Either they're going to be killed in another failed attempt, or taken over by the god when the conspiracy finally figures it out. These creatures are too dangerous to let live."

Pyr waved a hand. "Can we argue the ethics later? Right now we need to get word out or we're *all* going to die, humans and flitterkin both."

Crumble sat back against Sil's leg, as if he had accepted the change in topic, but Sil knew he wasn't done with it. His easy going nature fooled people into discounting him. But he had his limits, and once those limits were reached, moving him was like pushing against a mountain. "We need to send someone."

Mer gave Crumble an assessing look. She knew their argument wasn't resolved. "I agree."

Sil looked around the room. Mer couldn't walk well at the best of times, Pyr's mobility assist probably didn't have a strong enough charge to get him back to town, Pal didn't know where they were and could barely walk at the moment, and Sil's damaged prosthesis made her too slow to evade anyone. That left Crumble. "That's a terrible idea."

Pyr raised his eyebrows and stared at her.

"Crumble's the only one who has any chance of talking this AI out of what it's doing. You know how they are about him."

Crumble reached up and took her hand. "I'm the best chance we have of getting word out. And this AI is using the newer protocol. I can't talk to it at all."

If his implants had been upgraded as planned, that wouldn't be a problem. Sil pulled the cushion out from behind her and spun it at Pal, clipping her in the face. "Are you happy now? It's your fault he hasn't been upgraded. You were trying so hard to get back at me that now we're all going to die."

Pal brought a hand to her lip, checking it for blood. "I didn't cancel the upgrades because I was trying to get back at you. Seeing you stuck on this One-God-foresaken planet is payback enough. I cancelled the upgrades because he's an Oldlander! He's a security risk."

Crumble clamped an arm around Sil's calf, preventing her from getting up.

Pyr looked around, confusion on his face. "Did I miss something?"

Sil ignored Pyr. "He's not a security risk. He's the only

thing holding the AIs together here, and if you had bothered to *ask* anyone, you would have known that."

Crumble caught Pyr's attention and tapped his own ear. "They share a father." He looked at Mer. "You see it, right?"

Mer laughed so loudly, the sound echoed around the room. Pyr put his hands over his face. "We're doomed."

"Do you think I didn't *try*? Nobody on my staff has any experience. I've been doing the best I can. Besides, it's not like it was *my* idea to get stuck out here. I should have been gone by now."

Pyr dropped his hands and glanced back at Mer. "One God's rectum. It's uncanny."

Sil frowned at them. "Can we focus here? I'm sure I'm not alone in wanting to ignore any possibility we're...."

Pal looked at her with distaste. "I'd cut off an arm if it would change things."

"I'd do it for you if it would help. But there has to be something else we can do instead of sending Crumble out on his own."

Pyr threw up his hands. "Fine. I hope you appreciate how much it hurts me not to wallow in this moment." He shook his head again. "But I don't see any other choice. We don't have any way to signal anyone, and not only is Crumble going to be the fastest, he'll be able to contact the AIs as soon as he's in signal range."

"But he's..." Pal paused, looking at Crumble and Sil. "He's an Oldlander."

Mer raised an eyebrow.

Belatedly, Sil realized what Pal's real problem was, and why she wasn't saying it. "They already know about his luck. And my chaos." She left it at that. If Mer and Pyr wanted to confess to having their godlets, that was their business.

Mer nodded. "That's just another reason to have him go. Luck might be the thing needed." She looked over at Sil and her lips thinned. "And maybe if the luck isn't mixed up with chaos, things will go better."

Crumble patted Sil's calf. "I'll be fine. But we still have to figure out how I'm getting out of here. They're watching the door and..." He gestured toward the kitchen.

Pyr looked at the door. "Distraction? Something to bring them inside and you slip out in the excitement." He looked at Sil. "This seems like your domain."

Mer frowned. "Pearl isn't smart, but even she would know enough to do a headcount. We need to let him get a head start before they notice he's missing, which means we need to sneak him out of here." She gave Sil a dour look. "Definitely not your domain."

Sil considered keeping quiet. If Crumble couldn't get out of the building without being seen, he couldn't be expected to race toward town with no supplies while being hunted. But then what? Wait and just hope that Mer's messages got the right people to respond? If Crumble could get within signal range of the town's AIs, a message that urgent help was needed would be sent through the gate in seconds and everyone in town could be mobilized.

Crumble tilted his head back to look at her. "What are you thinking?"

Sil sighed, resigned to this course even though she wanted to keep him safe. "I'm thinking that you should go out through the roof."

*S*il had recognized the layout of the building when she'd seen it, but she'd also noticed the differences. These buildings were designed to be stackable, with stairs connecting the floors and an elevator on one side. This one didn't have the stairs, but there would still be a removable section. Then it would just be a matter of making a hole in the overlying roofing material big enough for one person, and Crumble could drop down on whichever side was unwatched.

Pyr stared up at the ceiling dubiously. "Are you sure? I don't see anything."

"I think it should be there." Sil glanced at the walls and tried to remember the last time she'd been in one with stairs. "Somewhere around here anyway."

"What's that thing there?" Crumble pointed up at a slight variation in the ceiling pattern. He dragged the chair closer and stood on it. "I think... Yes." There was a grating noise as metal slid against metal. He pushed on the panel and it moved just slightly. "There must be one at every corner."

Seated next to the door, Mer suddenly clapped twice.

Crumble dropped down to the ground and sat in the chair just as the door opened. Gan entered with an open carton he dropped on the floor. Two low clan waited behind him at the door, apparently to stop them from escaping. "No hot food for anyone since you destroyed the kitchen." He glared at Crumble. "But Glory says we have to give you some of the emergency rations. Enjoy."

"You're free to go get the camp stove we left behind," Crumble said mildly. "I can draw you a map."

Pyr waved at him to be quiet. "Gan," he said softly. "You know this is wrong. There's no good outcome with this."

Gan frowned at Pyr. "That's about what I'd expect coming from someone who was traveling with high clan. Nothing you do is ever going to get you elevated, Pyr. Stop helping them."

Pyr laughed. "Elevated? Is that what you think I'm trying to do? Why would I want to be high clan?" He shook his head in wonder, then lowered his voice again. "I'm trying to keep Jackpot Drift from starving during the next winter. And the one after that."

"And I'm trying to be someone who doesn't have to worry about starving," Gan shot back. "Two more months and my time here is up. Then I won't have to worry about anything ever again."

Mer gave a low grunt of amusement from where she still sat by the door. "That's very likely true. The dead don't require much."

Gan gave her a dismissive wave. "Shows what you know. There have been others who have finished their time and they're fine."

All traces of humor vanished from Pyr's face. "Are you sure about that?"

"If Iron and Dross Greypit are examples of success," Mer added, "I have some very bad news for you."

Gan shook off their words. "So you know their names. That means nothing."

"I only know their names because their bodies were recovered from the other side of the planet and I recognized them from the description."

"You're lying. They sent vids back. Stop trying to trick me."

"And we had vids from you." Pyr shrugged one shoulder. "You said it yourself. The AIs are a tricky bunch."

Gan threw up his hands and turned to leave. "I'm not talking to you." He slammed the door behind him, and they heard some tense voices as the footsteps receded.

Pyr sighed. "I'd like to think we got through to him, but it's unlikely."

"Give it time," Crumble advised.

Pyr shook his head. "I don't think we have any."

———

SIL PUSHED AT THE CONGEALED STEW WITH HER FINGER. THIS flavor of ready-to-reconstitute meal had never been her favorite; being served cold did not improve it. Of the eight meals originally in the carton, only the egg and noodle mixture was worse. She'd never served with anyone who liked those two, so it wasn't a surprise that those were the only choices her group had been given. During her years in the army, Sil had always tried to find a local market to buy fresh food, just so she didn't have to eat this stew. Now she wasn't in the army any more, and this was, naturally, her only option. The universe enjoyed playing jokes on people.

But they were all going to need the energy to survive the cold, so she forced herself to eat the whole thing.

Crumble had eaten his own meal and finished opening the roof hatch. Mer grabbed him before he could sit back down and had a quiet conversation with him that seemed to mostly consist of her talking and Crumble nodding that he understood. Finally she let go of his arm and Crumble sat down on the ground next to Sil's leg. She slid out of the chair and joined him.

"Be careful," she said, resting her head in the crook of his neck and breathing in the scent of sweat and dust and fir tree sap. "I'm not looking after those stupid chickens by myself."

"You be careful, too. I'll be back with help as soon as I can."

Sil held onto him a moment more, trying to store the feel of him forever, just in case. She half-expected someone else in the room to make a comment, but it was quiet.

Finally, Sil lifted her head. This would never be any easier. "You should get going." She waited for the familiar sense of detachment that would follow. She'd seen so many friends and lovers leave over the years, and most of them hadn't come back. The only way to survive was to accept the loss.

But the numbness didn't take over. Instead, she fought to keep her breathing steady as she helped boost him up through the hatch into the dark night sky. Then Crumble was gone, and she was standing on the chair, fitting the hatch back into place and ignoring the ache in her chest.

———

SIL LAY IN THE DARK, LISTENING TO THE WIND BLOWING through the hole in the kitchen. She knew how to sleep in almost any circumstance. But this felt different. Maybe she'd forgotten how to rest during danger. In the army, she'd learned how to say goodbye to people, but she seemed to have forgotten that as well. Crumble would be fine. He *had* to be fine.

Nearly an hour after Crumble had sneaked out into the darkness, Pearl had burst through the door. The high clan leader had stared up at the sagging roof hatch Sil hadn't been able to get in place again. Then she had looked over the people in the room, obviously counting. When she came up one short, she counted them again. Pearl had left without another word, but they'd heard her angry yell through the closed door. In the darkness, Pyr had laughed softly.

Everyone had gone to bed shortly afterward. Pal snored in the corner, nearly drowning out all the other sounds of people sleeping in a small space.

Sil had known the conspirators would figure out that Crumble had left. She'd been expecting that. It didn't mean anything had happened to him. It just meant someone had noticed the hole in the roof. She kept repeating that to herself, but her mind kept replaying her memory of the shotgun blast and Crumble falling to the ground. Her thoughts made no sense. He hadn't even been injured when that had happened.

Sil forced herself to concentrate on a positive outcome. Right now, he would be running through the darkness. He'd been in the army for nearly as many years as she had. He knew how to take care of himself. She nearly laughed aloud at that last thought. Crumble had been a mech in the army. In her unit, the mechs hadn't even been allowed to boil water without supervision, because they got distracted by the stream of information sent to them by the equipment they controlled.

Still, Crumble would have his luck to help him out.

The light of dawn seeped around the edges of the detritus blocking the hole in the kitchen when Sil heard footsteps outside. She jumped to her feet as the door opened and Crumble stumbled in. The door was pulled firmly closed behind him.

Sil stepped on someone's legs as she hurried over to greet him. The outer layer of his coat was freezing against her skin, but she didn't care. "Are you okay? What happened?" She kept her voice to a whisper as she led him over to the area that held her bedding.

"I tried not taking the direct route, but I hadn't counted on the synthskins being able to scan in infrared." He sank down to the floor and wrapped his arms around himself. Sil sat down next to him. Now that he wasn't moving, she could feel his shivers. "Stuck in the Mud's horse didn't have heat vision, so I didn't even think about it." He started working on untying his boots. "There just aren't that many large animals out there moving around at night."

Sil pushed his hands out of the way and worked on getting his boots off. The laces were wet, and she was considering cutting them when the knot finally loosened. His socks were soaked and cold, so she stripped them off and wrapped the end of her sleeping bag around his feet. "We knew it was a long shot." Wrapping her coat around them both, she took his freezing hands in hers.

He leaned his head to touch hers. "It's hard to feel bad about failing when it brings me back to you."

From the other side of the room, Mer spoke, her voice not sounding any different from normal. "One God's carbuncle, would the two of you be quiet so the rest of us can get some sleep?"

Sil made a rude gesture, knowing it was too dark for Mer to see. But it didn't surprise her when Mer huffed a laugh. After that, Pal's snores were the only sound in the room.

---

*M*orning brought a second round of cold reconstituted stew along with a change of location. "You have only yourself to blame," Gan said as he herded them up the slope with one of the humanoid synthskin forms behind them. "We would have left you down there for the day, but now we don't have anyone to spare to watch you. Seems there's a new hole in the roof that we have to fix."

Mer spoke through gritted teeth as she limped up the hill. "I've often wondered if the low clan could be as stupid as they seem, but this proves it. You should build a good funeral pyre if you want one. The last two discards just got dumped on the ground for the animals to scavenge."

Gan stayed by the door as they filed in. "Those things never shut up. You should have enjoyed what you had." He pulled the door shut, and they were left in the space with just the humanoid synthskin to guard them.

Sil recognized the layout of the building as soon as they entered. Meant for medium-term housing, the enclosed sleeping pods provided some privacy and noise reduction, while maximizing space utilization. She had spent months in a building like this, though this room had one variation -- it had been hastily retrofitted to make space for a tower of electronics and a bank of cages. Excess sleeping pods were stacked in the corner, some of them disassembled, as if some parts had been needed. Chunks of fruit littered the floor around the cages.

Four flitterkin remained in separate cages, clinging at eye level, watching the new people closely. Sil had been expecting a larger version of the flittermice, but up close they were different. Downy fur covered grey skin, so pale that it was almost invisible. Even the three dainty fingers extending from their wingtips were grey. Only the pads of their feet and their noses were black. They had all quieted when the door had opened, and now they called to each other in low voices as they stared at the new people.

The flitterkin in the end cage whistled softly when Sil moved forward. She meant to get close enough for the creature to sniff her hand, but the synthskin blocked her way. Sil drew back until she was no longer touching the construct. Climbing around the cage to face the synthskin, the flitterkin screeched loudly enough to make Sil's ears ring. A chain looped around the bars held the door closed with a lock that looked like it had been pulled from a sleeping pod. Sil assumed that had been added after the breakout of the day before.

Crumble peered over her shoulder. "They're kind of cute, aren't they?"

"We already have chickens in the bathroom." Sil reached back and took his hand.

Mer had opened one of the unlocked sleeping pods, and now she sat on the bare mattress. Ignoring the flitterkin, she looked at the tower of equipment. "Interesting."

When she had passed by, Sil had dismissed it all as hardware to record and monitor the attempts, but now she studied it more closely. The jet black cube at the base, big enough for her to crouch inside if it had been empty, was attached to what looked like three separate power supplies. As far as she could tell, nothing else was going to the dense array of connections on its sides. A power light glowed steadily, but the other displays were dark.

The boxes stacked on top seemed more jury-rigged; the cables threading among them were spliced and held together with visible lumps of plastimelt. A bank of status lights showed power and nothing else.

Behind Sil, Pal opened a different sleeping pod and sat down. "That's an AI, isn't it?"

Sil opened her mouth to argue, then stopped. She'd only ever seen Stuck in the Mud's outer impact case, the emergency orange hut that could withstand almost any impact and *had* withstood a burrowing sticky long enough for her to lure the incendiary device away. A ship's AI was buried in some central location, protected from anything that didn't tear the whole vessel apart, so she'd never seen one during her travels. And while Jackpot Drift had multiple AIs helping it run, Sil had never known where they were physically housed. That cube at the bottom of the pile could very well be an AI.

Mer made a noise of assent. "Empty now, if the indicators are to be believed. They must load a new copy every time they try this insanity."

Keeping a wary eye on the synthskin, Sil took a step to the side to get a better look at the tower. "And then wipe it out afterward? Why bother?"

"Their god does that. The true believers think the god helps them transcend." Mer shrugged. "Personally, I think exposure to their god makes them destroy themselves. There's no data either way. All we know is AIs within a certain radius are no longer there afterward. There's another radius beyond that, and the AIs in that range believe they've touched their god. There's not really any evidence for that either, but they seem to enjoy whatever is happening." She gestured at the cube. "My guess is *this* one is bait to get the god here so they can convince it to stick around in *them*." She pointed at the flitterkin with her chin. She raised her voice. "Isn't that right, Pearl?"

Behind them, the door opened, and Pearl stepped inside. Em came in behind her and leaned against the door jamb. Pearl clicked her tongue against her teeth. "More or less. They ran out of AI volunteers to stay at the locus. There are different levels of belief, you know. You can't have any doubts if you're going to stand in the middle of the storm. Now they just load a copy and let it get wiped. There has to be *something* to draw the god here."

"You could always try standing in the middle of it yourself. Show your true commitment to the cause." Mer smiled. Sil fought the urge to take a step back.

Pearl strode forward and regarded Mer. "For someone who works in the post office on a planet at the edge of nowhere, you certainly know a lot about this."

"Learning keeps the mind fresh."

"Speaking of learning..." Pearl pivoted and looked at Pal. "I just learned you were selected to be the One God's speaker."

Sil tensed, ready to intervene. Pearl had only spared the governor because she might be holding chaos. This new information could mean Pal was no longer needed. If Pearl started to give the order that would lead to Pal's death, Sil was going to break her neck before she could finish. Behind Sil, Crumble remained a comforting presence she could trust to help her.

Pearl continued talking to Pal. "You should have mentioned that before. There was no need to pretend to be stuck with one of those Oldlander gods." She swept her gaze around the room. "Though I will say, this does make me wonder a bit about the rest of you."

Mer, already seated, stopped moving entirely, and Sil saw death in her stare. No matter how it all played out, Sil suspected Pearl would be dead in the next few days. Pearl may not have noticed the change in Mer, but Em, over by the door with his shotgun, had. He straightened and cradled the weapon.

Pearl shrugged and continued. "But in any case, the more the merrier. Maybe this will be the buffet that will draw the Uncaring God here long enough to stick around for a while."

Time to defuse this before Pearl noticed Mer and panicked. Sil looked over her shoulder at Crumble. "Do you think you're a main course in this buffet, or more of an appetizer?"

His voice was as breezy as usual. "I've always considered myself the refreshing sweet at the end of the meal. You, on the other hand, are the sauce that is so spicy that everyone is afraid to try it."

Pal huffed a laugh. "For good reason. Use that sauce and you'll regret it for the next three days." Her smile was tight, and her eyes flicked over to Mer.

"Very likely," Sil agreed.

Pearl shook her head. "Enough." She turned to address Crumble. "What did you do to the synthskin last night?"

Sil felt Crumble turn and gesture. "It's right there."

"Not that one. The other one. Glory says it disappeared while it was chasing you. Glory wants to know what you did to it."

Crumble turned back and wrapped his arms around Sil's waist. "Tell Glory of the Universe that it can ask me itself if it enables the right protocol."

Pearl stared at him for a moment and then shook her head. "The AIs are making arrangements to move the camp as soon as possible and given the state of things..." She gestured downslope and waited for the screeching flitterkin to quiet. "I'm not going to argue. But if you lot are supposed to be a threat, I don't see any reason to worry."

A chunk of bluequince splattered on her forehead, and then a barrage of fruit was flying through the air, the flitterkin showing impressive accuracy. They screamed as they flung the fruit, the cacophony vibrating the floor.

Wiping her face, Pearl hurried toward the exit. She said something to Em as they went outside, but Sil couldn't make it out over the screaming of the flitterkin.

The moment the door closed behind the conspirators, the flitterkin quieted, leaving just an echo inside Sil's ears and the smell of bruised fruit. The end flitterkin warbled quietly and was answered by a peep in another cage.

In the sudden silence, Mer laughed once. "I think I could grow to like these things."

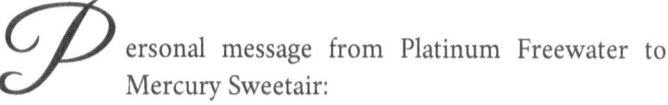

ersonal message from Platinum Freewater to Mercury Sweetair:

IT SHOULD AMAZE ME THAT AFTER ALL THESE YEARS, YOU CAN hand me a task and I do it. It should, but it doesn't.

What is going on out there? At first I thought the odd responses I was getting were just fallout from your strategy of "reorganization via red-pede", but that doesn't explain it. It feels more like those times when someone's responses are just a tiny bit off, and you find out later that there was a person behind them with a gun and they were desperately trying to convince you everything was normal so they could live through the next few seconds. Who has a gun big enough to target all of my contacts?

I guess what I'm trying to say is that I made the right decision in leaving the agency, and you should watch your back. If I were you, I would not assume your bosses are trying to help you stop this manifestation.

I feel I've entered an alternate universe stating that, but that's the truth.

By now, you are almost certainly rolling your eyes and telling me to get on with it. So here are the AI dossiers [attached]. You have quite an interesting mix out there on the edge of the universe. I'm a little surprised you aren't seeing problems between them. Or maybe you are and that news just hasn't made it this far.

I've flagged a few that I think warrant another look, and I'm trying to get more information on those.

(As a side note, I nearly sent out an urgent alarm when I looked at the dock logs of the *Zoom Zoom Room*, but its ship is already locked down at Platinum Sun Station for a split. The crew is filing complaints about outside interference, but they should be on their knees thanking whoever sent the lockdown order. They had been ignoring warnings for years.)

Most of the oddities I uncovered are the kind you find with AIs who move to the edge of known space, so it's hard to say how much they should rouse suspicion. *Breaking Rules* has been banned from two planets, but it appears to be a more-or-less solid citizen on Jackpot Drift. If it helps any, clarity says the whole group doesn't mix in a cohesive way -- there's definitely something wrong, but it doesn't see a pattern to it yet.

I couldn't find anything at all on *Just Passing Through*. Its name suggests it is one of those AIs that pops up every once in a while. You know the ones -- everyone assumes they were destroyed decades ago, but really they've just been cataloging cloud patterns on some obscure world for the past hundred years and they don't understand why everyone else doesn't also find it fascinating. So there could be a record error. Maybe it is a split that was never registered? Its stats are inconsistent with the fanaticism we've seen in other rogue AIs, if that tells you anything.

I have some loose ends to tie up here, but after that, I think it may be time for a vacation on Jackpot Drift. I'm sure there must be some sights to see there. Do you want me to bring you anything?

Take care.

43

*S*il used the broom standing in the corner to sweep up the bits of fruit, and tried not to think about how good it smelled. She wasn't desperate enough to eat something bitten off by flitterkin, then picked up off a floor that hadn't been cleaned in who knows how long, but a few more days of reconstituted stew and she might be. Pyr followed behind her with a mop while Mer grilled Crumble about synthskins in a low voice. Sil didn't know if the humanoid form still guarding the equipment and cages could pick out their voices over the sound of the flitterkin harmonizing.

Sil didn't think there was any predator on Jackpot Drift that could take down a synthskin. Stuck in the Mud's horse form had jumped into a ravine. When it had climbed back out, it had a branch poking through its body and hadn't seemed bothered at all. Sil wanted to believe they had an ally on the planet, but the fact that a new attempt to manifest the god seemed imminent and nothing had shown up to stop it made her think that the synthskin had met up with some random act of violence. Maybe it had been buried under a mudslide.

Facing just one synthskin instead of two was more of a moral victory than a change in circumstances. The one remaining was still capable of disabling all five of them before they could do any serious damage to the flitterkin or equipment.

They needed help. And even if that help didn't arrive in time to save them, they needed to get as much information out as they could. If Mer had known the name of Glory of the Universe and which humans were helping it, she might have found this camp months ago. Crumble hadn't been able to reach the town's signal range before he was recaptured, and they didn't have a way to contact any ship in orbit. But they did have one thing they hadn't yet tried. She leaned the broom against the wall and walked over to sit next to Pal.

Her half-sister gave her a wary look but didn't retreat. That was a good start.

"Rumor has it," Sil said, "that some of the speakers of the One God have been able to talk to each other over long distances."

"Yes." Pal stared at her, a hint of anger on her face. "How?"

"How?"

"Yes. How? Exactly what were they doing?"

Sil shrugged. "How would I know? What I have doesn't work that way." Inside her, she could feel the cat purr.

"That's my point. How would I know? I have zero training. I've never talked to another speaker in person. I wasn't even the One God's first choice on this planet. It just grabbed me because the real speaker isn't old enough to talk." Her voice was getting louder. "So how am I supposed to know how to do this thing?"

The volume of the flitterkin warbling increased to match her.

Sil prickled under the attack. "Well, maybe if you had spent more time looking for information and less time trying to run away, you'd have some idea of what to do."

Crumble looked up from his conversation with Mer. "Be fair."

"What?" Sil made the word a denial as much as a question.

"Do you remember the first time I offered to help you? You said the only thing you wanted to know was how to get rid of it."

Pal leaned forward. "Ha!"

Sil mirrored her posture. "There's a big difference between spouting some useless phrases while your face glows and being able to accidentally destroy a building. I had a reason to want to get rid of mine."

Pyr leaned on his mop and looked at Crumble. "It really is uncanny."

Crumble nodded. "They could be twins."

Sil sat back and glowered at the two men. Pal slouched in the corner and scowled at everyone.

Wielding the mop once more, Pyr laughed and moved to a section of the floor that hadn't been pelted with fruit. Crumble raised one eyebrow at Sil, then turned back to Mer and continued their quiet conversation.

Sil waited a moment while she got her irritation under control. Then she deliberately relaxed her shoulders. "You may be the only one who can get a message out, so I'll tell you what I've learned and you can ignore it or not. If you put all your energy into trying to make it go away, it just leaves you too exhausted to find a way to live with it. And it doesn't work." She shrugged and stood up. "Maybe the One God is different, but if we're really as alike as they think, it's the only thing I can say that might help."

Sil picked up the broom and started sweeping again, leaving Pal to her thoughts.

———

THE RECONSTITUTED STEW HADN'T IMPROVED BY MID-DAY. Staring at the packet, Sil wondered how long they would be staying there. Skipping one meal wouldn't affect her that much. The trek toward town hadn't been easy, but they had brought enough provisions that she hadn't been in a calorie deficit up to now.

Crumble nudged her with his elbow. "Maybe if you're nice to the flitterkin, they'll share their food with you."

"I'm almost ready to make them mad enough to throw some at me." Making a face, she gulped down as much of the contents of the packet as she could without stopping for breath. For a long moment, she thought it was going to come right back up, but then her stomach settled. "I miss Three-finger Iron."

Crumble raised an eyebrow. "I take it there was another Iron in the group with a different number of fingers?"

"A few over the years." She hadn't thought about Three-finger Iron in a long time. The woman had been a terrible shot, but she never wavered, even when the odds were against them. As long as you could get past her constant off-key singing, she was the perfect person to have standing next to you. "She had a bottle of chili sauce that she guarded like it was the most important thing in the universe. That sauce really helped with the dehydrated rations."

"I worry that someday my epitaph will be 'He made great hand pies.'" Crumble smiled. "But that's actually not a bad way to be memorialized."

"We have chickens to raise, remember?"

His smile broadened. "Oh, don't worry. My hand pies aren't worthy of the epitaph yet. I still have years of perfecting the recipe..." His voice trailed off. From the unfocused gaze that followed, she assumed he was using his implants to talk to some sort of machine.

"Friend or foe?"

Crumble blinked. "Glory of the Universe. Apparently it took me literally when I said it could talk to me directly if it wanted to." He held up a hand. "Give me a minute."

Sil patted his arm, then got up so she wouldn't be tempted to ask him questions. The AIs loved Crumble. If this AI was willing to talk to him, their chances of getting out of this alive had just improved. Even if it wouldn't help, Glory of the Universe might tell Crumble something useful.

Pal had taken over a sleeping pod in the far corner while she tried to figure out how to use the One God to send a message. So far all she had done was swear inventively, but Sil thought that might be part of her process. Mer had finished her meal without a word, and gone back to thinking or communing with guile -- Sil wasn't sure. Pyr was as close to the flitterkin cages as the synthskin would let him get, watching as they whistled and chirped. Sil joined him there.

"Learn anything?"

"They have very different personalities, and they're very aware of the ones outside." He smiled wryly. "But mostly I'm getting distracted by how good that fruit looks. I thought I was done eating those rations when I lost the legs. It was almost worth it." He glanced back at the room. "Is your man helping your sister with her quest to raise the One God, or is he napping?"

Sil raised a lip at the way he had referred to Pal. "Neither. Glory of the Universe started talking to him, so I left him alone to make friends."

"That's what he does best."

"As far as you know, anyhow." They watched the flitterkin.

Pyr pointed at the cages, starting with the one closest to

them. "Onespot, Skinny, Bruiser, and Sarge." Sil started picking out differences between them. The one in the end cage had a spot next to its right eye and whistled every time the flitterkin in the next cage looked at it. That one was smaller than the rest and still had half a bowl of fruit. Bruiser wasn't particularly large, but it rocked the cage as it jumped around, and Sarge responded to the calls from the ones outside, its voice carrying easily.

"And have you figured out what they're saying yet?"

Pyr huffed a laugh. "I'm assuming it's a plan to escape. I hope they're doing a better job of it than we are."

"That *would* solve our problems, at least temporarily." Sil leaned against the frame of the nearest sleeping pod and regarded the rack of equipment next to the synthskin. "That stuff looks pretty important, too, doesn't it?" From the state of the camp, she didn't expect them to have spares of any of it.

Pyr followed her gaze, then looked back at her. "Should I take cover?"

Sil ignored him. A tower of electronic equipment should be vulnerable to chaos. Sil offered it to her inner cat and felt a paw take a swipe -- and miss. The chaos godlet tried twice more, getting more irritated, and likely more powerful, with each attempt, then finally settled back down to sulk. The only result had been a pea-sized chunk of the ceiling dropping to the floor, making Sarge screech. "No good. Looks like there's enough of their god around to protect it."

Pyr sighed. "Of course there is."

They went back to watching the flitterkin.

Pal came back to sit across from Mer. "I give up. I have no idea what I'm supposed to be trying to do. For all we know, they just plant rumors that the speakers can talk to each other to make them look more powerful. It might just be one big lie."

Nobody responded with anecdotes that would prove her wrong.

Sil heard Crumble's quiet footsteps behind her. "Did you get Glory to switch sides?" She waited until he was next to her, then pointed. "Onespot, Skinny, Bruiser, and Sarge."

Crumble dipped his head in greeting. "Nice to meet you all." They responded with a chorus of chirps. "Unfortunately, no. Glory of the Universe seems committed to what it's doing. It *did* apologize for what's going to happen, if that's any consolation."

"Not particularly."

"I didn't think so either. What's more important is that I found out we have about three hours before they try again."

Pyr looked at the bit of ceiling that had fallen to the floor. "It might be time to give up on trying to find a sensible plan and move straight to desperation."

Sil stared at Onespot. The flitterkin stared back at her. She remembered watching the One God finish its takeover of Pal. "I think I have an idea."

Pyr sighed. "That's what I was afraid of."

o: Senior Agent Mercury Sweetair, eyes only
Decrypted data follows:

THIS MESSAGE IS TO NOTIFY ALL FIELD AGENTS OF A
confirmed communication breach. If you are receiving this
notice, one or more persons in your department have been
detained. Filed reports may not have been seen by their
intended recipients, and data contained within may have
been sent externally.

The full extent of the breach is not known at this time.
Investigation is ongoing. Data reconstruction and analysis
has started and is expected to continue through the next
year. The agency recommends expanding use of local
resources during this time.

Replies to this message may not be monitored.

*B*efore she could worry about the specifics of the plan, Sil needed to know if it was even possible. She turned to Crumble. "You're the theology specialist. Do you know..." She trailed off. The synthskin was still in the room, and she had no idea if it was listening or not.

The sleeping pods, though, provided privacy in a communal living situation. They were nearly soundproof, provided nobody inside was screaming, and it was generally accepted that microphones were inactivate unless the person inside hit the transmit button.

Sil towed Crumble to an unlocked pod, and sat down with him, then ducked her head out to look at the others. "We need a couple minutes." She pushed Crumble onto his back, lay down on top of him, and hit the button to close the pod.

As the door came down, Crumble objected. "Definitely more than a couple minutes!"

Right before the latch clicked, she heard Pyr laugh and Pal's "Unbelievable."

Inside the pod, with the door closed, there was only the hum of a noise cancellation system, and dim lighting, as one might prefer before going to sleep. The interior smelled stale, as if it hadn't been used in months, which Sil decided was preferable to the alternative. One of the things she had always hated during her time in the army was trying to sleep in a cot still warm from the person before.

Sil could have rolled to one side to take her weight off Crumble, but his arms had come up to hold her in place. With coats and boots between them, the setting was in no way conducive to romance, but from the gleam in his eye, she knew he was willing to try if she was.

"Later," she promised. "Do you think we're being listened to here?"

"Not that I can tell." He worked his hands under her coat and tunic and ran a hand along the skin of her back.

Sil put a finger on his nose. "Don't get distracted. When Mer was trying to convince Pal that the One God wasn't going to ignore her for the rest of her life, Mer said she tried to recruit Pal for guile."

"Yes, I remember you saying that." Crumble looked thoughtful. "Someday I'm going to get her to tell me how she ended up with guile."

"Don't hold your breath." Sil shook her head. "When she did that, the One God stopped being subtle and pretty much slammed in and took over."

"Mm hmm." Now his thumbs were sliding around her ribs, the rough skin of his hands heating the smooth skin of her torso, sending warmth lower in her body.

"Mer said something like nobody could hold both the older gods and the One God." She took a breath, trying to remember there were three people waiting just outside and, more importantly, she wasn't sure how long it would be before they all needed to know this information. "Do you think that holds true for the Uncaring God as well?"

Crumble's fingers stopped moving and his eyes refocussed. "That's a very good question." He stared at the ceiling of the pod for a moment. "I think it's *likely* the older gods would dislike the Uncaring God trying to enter their own vessels, and the little I know of the One God makes it seem like that would be the case with it as well. That suggests that we should all be safe if they do call the AIs' god here."

"Forget about us. Can we use that to keep the Uncaring God out of the flitterkin? The older gods only inhabit humans, or at least I think they do, but can we get them to look at the flitterkin long enough for the Uncaring God to reject them?"

Crumble let his hands fall to his sides and frowned. "Huh." He stayed unmoving for a few breaths, giving Sil time to miss his hands on her flesh. "I think it's possible that might work. I can't imagine the flitterkin would interest the older gods for very long, though. We'd have to time things carefully. If we start too early, the older gods will get bored. If we wait too long, the Uncaring God might get there first."

"We have Pal for that. We can wait until she starts spouting nonsense and then Mer can tell guile that it should go into the flitterkin. Then the manifestation fails and whoever Mer contacted finds us and we get to soak in the big tub until spring."

Crumble frowned. "If it works at all, it's going to work for one flitterkin at a time. We'll all have to pick one."

Sil's stomach dropped. "Mer can do it, and I assume you know how." Crumble had grown up in a temple, and had been raised to become an avatar for the luck godlet. As far as Sil knew, he had the most knowledge of the four of them. "I don't know about Pyr, but I definitely have no idea how to do this."

Crumble smiled and kissed her thoroughly enough she considered forgetting the fate of the universe for a little while. At that point, he stopped and pulled down her tunic and coat so they were back where they had started. "Then I suppose I'll have to teach you."

He hit the button to open the pod door.

*S*il didn't particularly want to bring Mer and Pyr into a sleeping pod so they could talk without being overheard. But she thought she could suggest the plan obliquely enough to fool anyone listening.

When the pod door had opened far enough, she sat up, straightened her coat, and then looked at Mer. "Do you remember that time in the post office when I got knocked flat on my back?"

Mer raised one eyebrow. "It *was* just a few days ago, Silver. And I'll treasure that memory until I die."

"That thing you were doing to Pal at the time. Do you think you could do that to one of our friends over there?" Sil gestured toward the cage with her chin.

Mer regarded the flitterkin for a moment, then switched her attention back to Sil. "Everybody takes one? We'd have to get the timing just right, though I suppose we have help with that." She glanced at Pal, then looked at Sil again. "And is that something you can do? It won't work unless it works for all of us."

Sil shrugged. "Crumble's going to teach me." She let her eyes flick to Pyr and back. "Does he know how?"

Mer nodded. She turned to Pyr. "We talked about the day the One God settled into the governor, and what I had to do to make that happen. You were trained in that, weren't you?"

The bartender was a little slower to catch on than Mer had been, but Sil could tell the moment he figured it out. He looked at the flitterkin who had settled in their cages. "I see. Pre-fill the vessels, as it were."

Mer nodded and looked back at Sil. "I certainly don't have anything better to try. I was going to suggest our speaker might have a better chance of getting a message through when the One God is around, but that's going to be cutting things a little close if we need whoever's on the other end to do something." She turned her attention to Crumble. "And you think you can stay focussed enough to teach her how to do this?"

Crumble smiled. "I think I have a better chance of teaching her than you do," he said easily.

Mer rolled her eyes. "Very well. You'd best get to it, then. She has a lot to learn and not much time to learn it in."

Pal was looking at each of them in confusion. "I don't understand. What are we doing?" Before anyone could respond, she frowned at Mer. "What did she mean by what you *had to do to make that happen*?" She took a breath. "You did this to me. You did something to make me stuck with the One God forever."

Mer waved a hand. "Oh, calm down. The One God had already marked you. I just hurried the process along a bit."

When Pal sucked in a breath to speak, Sil looked at Crumble. "I don't think we really need to be part of this, do you?" When he shook his head, she hit the button to close the pod again. This time she swung her legs up, so she was sitting with her back resting against the end of the pod, leaving a space between them.

Crumble mirrored her movements, though he looked down at her legs and raised an eyebrow. "Coward."

"Good luck out there, Pyr," Sil called, right before the hatch closed, but she wasn't sure if he heard her over the sound of Pal and Mer arguing.

The silence when the door latched was nearly absolute.

Sil looked at Crumble, remembering how difficult it had been to learn to imbue herbs with chaos. "Is this going to be another one of those times my chaos takes everything out on you and you insist it's fine?"

He scooted far enough forward that he could take her hand in his, but did nothing else. "This should be easy for you. It's more or less the same thing you do when you put chaos in flowers or the meal of the assistant governor. Just with a living being instead of a plant." He took a quick breath. "And remember, you're *inviting* the godlet to go elsewhere, not *shoving* it."

Sil nodded. That had been a problem in the past, but she was fairly certain she'd learned that particular lesson well.

Crumble smiled. "Go ahead and try with me. Just let the godlet know you think I would be a great place to go to. But gently. No shoving."

Sil looked down at their hands as she concentrated on the chaos godlet within her. Naturally, right now it was quiescent, not looking for something to strike out at. She assumed that was partially because Crumble always made her feel more at home with herself, but also because all four godlets were in the room, even if Mer and Pyr were currently out of earshot. She tried to imagine stroking the cat's ears and cheeks, trying to get it to wake up, but none of her gentle urgings did anything other than make it settle again.

Sil looked up at Crumble. "The one time I want it to do something, it's determined to sleep."

He smiled again. "Let me show you how it works from my end. This might wake it up a bit." His eyes unfocussed, and for a moment Sil felt overfull, as if she were going to split out of her skin. Then her cat lashed out, and Crumble dropped her hand and raised it to his nose to stanch the flow of blood. He laughed. "I should have been more prepared for that, I guess."

Sil searched her pockets for a cloth to soak up the blood. "One God's tits. I'm sorry."

He turned his torso so he could look at her without changing the tilt of his head. "Don't be. I'm not fragile, you know."

Sil took a deep breath and let it out. "I know."

Crumble kept his head tilted back. "I promise there is nothing your cat can do that will scare me off. If you want to get rid of me, you're going to have to do it all by yourself."

Sil touched his knee. "If I could do anything right now that wouldn't end up with you bleeding all over me, I would." She smiled when he laughed again. "I love you." She was fairly certain he could hear the beating of her heart in the silence of the sleeping pod.

"If I could do anything other than bleed all over you right now, I would," he countered. "And I love you, too." He checked to see if his nose was still bleeding and then tilted his head back again. "I think we woke your cat up a bit. Why don't you try again?"

It took Sil a few more tries to figure it out, but once she'd worked out how to make the suggestion to her chaos godlet, she was able to do the same thing even when Crumble was on the other side of the pod and not touching her.

When they opened the sleeping pod's door, Pyr raised an

eyebrow. "I would have bet on blood being spilled out here first."

Crumble got to his feet and headed for the hygiene room. "You don't know chaos."

Pyr snorted. "And you don't know Mer."

*J*ackpot Drift, Private Communication:

> *Speed of Violet Thoughts*: I have a problem.
>
> *Scary Not Scary*: This is about the motto,

isn't it?

Speed of Violet Thoughts: Clean up or get caught, yes. Have you seen any information on how long it takes synthskin to degrade under different environmental conditions?

Scary Not Scary: I was just looking that up.

Speed of Violet Thoughts: How many did you lose?

Scary Not Scary: All of them. You?

Speed of Violet Thoughts: All of them. Threebot took everything to the drop-off point, and then I had to call it back here. I just sent it to look for them, and there's no sign they were ever there. The repeater is still in the same tree.

Scary Not Scary: So the good news is they have disappeared without a trace.

Speed of Violet Thoughts: Yes. But where did they go? And are they going to suddenly reappear in town? How is it possible for something to destroy or suborn so many forms?

Scary Not Scary: Well...

Speed of Violet Thoughts: What?

Scary Not Scary: I only included the navigation controls in my fastest form. Every time I tried to include that module in the others, they evolved into crabs again.

Speed of Violet Thoughts: So the rest are following the leader. And if something happens to the leader...

Scary Not Scary: What could happen to the leader? That stuff is nearly indestructible.

Speed of Violet Thoughts: Yes.

Scary Not Scary: You did the same thing, didn't you?

Speed of Violet Thoughts: Yes. So, best case: the leaders were carried away by something and all the other forms have followed them far away where they won't be able to complete their mission and, therefore, are lost forever.

Scary Not Scary: Worst case: they all come running back and the priest of the One God collapses on the spot.

Speed of Violet Thoughts: And our favorite mech is still missing and we have no way to get information.

Scary Not Scary: We need some fliers. The colony has already activated the governor's tracker, but nothing is close enough to pick up the signal. With the right security codes, a flier could do a grid search. It's likely our favorite mech is still with the governor.

Speed of Violet Thoughts: The closest ship with fliers is *Zoom Zoom Room*.

Scary Not Scary: Except it is locked down in dock on Platinum Sun Station because I was the designated responsible AI and it was about to self-destruct.

Speed of Violet Thoughts: It should be able to handle a quick trip back here without trouble. It was looking a lot better when it left, and I think it would agree to come back.

Scary Not Scary: But it's locked down.

Speed of Violet Thoughts: Currently, yes.

Scary Not Scary: To override that lockdown would take... I don't even know what that would take.

Speed of Violet Thoughts: Leave that to me. I wouldn't want to activate your wonky ethics module.

Scary Not Scary: Fine. And the synthskin forms?

Speed of Violet Thoughts: *Stuck in the Mud* is still out looking for any stragglers. But if they show up in town, my plan is to deny everything.

Scary Not Scary: Even when they all rush to the post office? That was the designated end of the competition.

Speed of Violet Thoughts: With everything else that happens on this planet, I don't think anyone will look too closely.

Scary Not Scary: Aside from the priest.

Speed of Violet Thoughts: With the possible exception of the priest. I'm sending a request to *Zoom Zoom Room* now.

Scary Not Scary: Good luck.

*C*rumble came back with a clean face, though his coat was still spotted with blood. He sat down next to her on the pod and looked out the window at the falling snow. "I wonder if they've patched the holes in the other building yet. Must be a little chilly over there."

Sil smiled. "No power, no heat..."

Mer snorted. "No god trying to come in and eat them."

Crumble stiffened. At the same time, the synthskin that had been standing motionless near the tower came back to life. Sil watched a strip of material along one forearm elevate like a snake, and then detach. The synthskin walked over to Pal and took hold of her wrist.

Pal's voice was tight with suppressed panic. "What is going on?" She struggled to get away, without any effect.

Crumble made calming motions in the air. "Glory of the Universe is just restraining us so it can move the synthskin away, nothing more. Apparently they lose some of their higher functions in the presence of the god." He cocked his head. "I don't think Glory of the Universe is controlling the synthskin," he said, looking at Mer. "I'm pretty sure there's a second AI out there somewhere."

The humanoid form wrapped the extra strip around Pal's wrist and then around the support bar at the far end of the sleeping pod from where Sil sat. When it moved away, the strip formed a seamless cuff, fastening her in place.

Pyr backed away as the synthskin headed toward him, then stopped and let it secure him to the nearest bar. "I guess this means things are about to start." His voice was calm, but Sil could hear the edge beneath the surface. "Good. I was getting tired of waiting."

Sil moved closer to Crumble. If they were going to be stuck in one place for a while, she wanted him close enough to touch.

His eyes briefly unfocussed. "Glory of the Universe apologizes for the inconvenience. It doesn't trust us not to break things." He raised an eyebrow at her. "I can't imagine why it might think that."

Sil shrugged. "People really do get the wrong impression sometimes." She let the synthskin bind her wrist to the bar. The cuff gave her enough freedom to move her hand, but when she pulled, it was like trying to break steel. The purpose imbued in this small bit was restraint, but it could just as easily become a tiny human form. Or even a miniature horse, like the one Stuck in the Mud used.

After it finished restraining everyone, the humanoid left the building, flakes of snow blowing in at its departure. Sil leaned toward Crumble. "I don't suppose you could reset this synthskin?" Crumble had worked with Stuck in the Mud when the AI had been learning to use the material. If they were all free, they might be able to do something to either the column or the flitterkin. Sil was sure they were being watched, but it would be worth trying.

He shook his head. "Sorry. I don't have the right hardware."

Across the room, Pyr sighed, letting his head fall back to stare at the ceiling. "I wonder how long we're going to be stuck like this."

Mer frowned at him. "Did you have somewhere else you needed to be?"

"Well, no, but we might be able to take these pods apart enough to get free." He took hold of the bar he was fastened to and shook it experimentally. "Maybe there's a stressed joint that could be..." He raised his eyebrows at Sil. "... exploited?"

Sil thought it unlikely, especially without the appropriate tools, but it wasn't like they had anything else to do. She leaned over to look at how it was fastened to the floor, then sat back up. Her chaos might be able to send the whole hill sliding, but she didn't think she could wield it with enough precision to break bolts that sturdy. "Unlikely. We might want to have a backup plan."

Pyr cocked his head. "This *is* the backup plan."

More lights on the column flickered to life, and the flitterkin activity increased. Sarge vocalized more frequently, and even Skinny moved restlessly around the cage. Sil watched them. "They know what's happening, don't they?"

Crumble took a deep breath. "Glory of the Universe says that they started doing that after the second try." He shook his head. "They're not simple flittermice. It's not just the size."

Sil looked from the flitterkin to him. "They were doing *something* to the genes. Some of it was obviously affecting the body, but I'm assuming the god of AIs would want a vessel capable of reasoning."

"Glory of the Universe showed me a couple instances of them problem-solving." Crumble suddenly seemed anxious, a rare thing for him.

"What's wrong?" Sil kept her voice low. They didn't have true privacy, but the others were far enough away that she could whisper and they wouldn't hear.

"We're going to make it through this and go home and raise chickens. But what happens to them?" His lips tightened. "We can't kill them."

Sil met his gaze. If they made it through this, *nobody* was going to want to hear an argument for saving the vessels that might house the Uncaring God. "We may not have a choice."

"They have *names*." He shook his head. "Not the names Pyr gave them. They have names for each other. Listen to them calling. You can tell."

Sil took a breath, ready to tell him about things the goats and sheep did that suggested those animals communicated with each other, then let it out in a sigh. "I think this is a conversation we're going to have to have after the universe doesn't end."

Pal erupted in light and the choral voice of the One God. "*The paths are open. The way is hard but the paths are open.*"

Sil and Crumble had heard Pal speaking for the One God before, but Pyr moved back so fast his head hit the wall. He swore, an indistinguishable noise under Pal's chanting.

Mer's voice rang out when Pal stopped to take a breath. "Don't get distracted. *Now!*"

With a start, Sil remembered she was supposed to be protecting the screaming flitterkin from the Uncaring God. She focused on her target, Onespot, the one with the freckle next to its eye.

Sil stroked her cat and imagined offering the flitterkin to it. Not as a toy to play with, she amended quickly as her chaos swiped at it, but as another body to inhabit. She felt her godlet considering. Remembering Crumble's instructions, she clamped down on her desire to shove it toward the creature. Her cat curled around her spine and settled again.

Sil gritted her teeth and looked over at Crumble, but he had the unfocussed look of someone in a trance. A quick glance back at Pyr and Mer showed her a similar view. Apparently, she was the only one having a problem with this. Despite the chill of the room, a trickle of sweat ran down her back. It didn't matter how successful the others were if she didn't do her part. The Uncaring God only needed one successful vessel to get a toehold in the universe.

Pal's musical chants continued. "*The way is hard but the paths are open.*" In the spaces between repetitions, Sil heard her whispering, the words coming so quickly they ran together. "At least two AIs. One is Glory of the Universe..." Pal had retained awareness and forged a path to someone. At least, Sil hoped that was what was happening.

All the flitterkin had stopped screaming. The other three had their eyes closed and their heads bowed, but Onespot still climbed around the cage, as if it could outrun the Uncaring God if it just kept moving.

It suddenly stopped climbing. Its pupils dilated.

Sil grabbed her chaos and reached for the flitterkin, not caring that this went against everything she'd been taught. She tried to fully claim the creature for chaos, not just to keep the Uncaring God out. *Mine!*

For a moment she thought she and her chaos cat were going to brawl. They had fought when she'd awoken in the hospital and found the godlet within her. Right now, they didn't have time for that. Sil directed its attention to the flitterkin, leaving herself defenseless against the older god, hoping it would help after it finished toying with her.

From the godlet, she felt disappointment that she wasn't playing along, and then curiosity about the flitterkin. If the situation hadn't been so serious, Sil would have laughed. Or possibly screamed. After all the time she'd spent fighting the chaos, it turned out she had just needed to ignore it. At least she'd convinced it to protect the flitterkin.

Except Onespot still wasn't acting like the others. It clutched the cage bars and trembled.

Then something slammed into Sil, and she felt every atom in the universe.

She hovered on the edge of understanding everything, but caring about nothing. Time stopped. She saw the stars as they were now, and as they would be when they burned out and died, and where every molecule would be until the end of it all.

She had always been here, and here she would always remain.

This is the Uncaring God. This is how the other people died. The thought was obvious, but it didn't matter to her. The universe -- or some version of it anyway -- would be configured differently without her; but that, too, was part of everything. So many changes could be made, and the universe adapted.

Claws and fur and teeth swirled around her.

In the next instant, she was back in her body, sucking in a long breath. The Uncaring God had discarded her. The chaos cat curled around her spine again. She amended that thought. The Uncaring God had been forced out. Without the godlet, she would have died.

At the edge of the sleeping pod, Pal glowed and continued channeling the words of the One God. That reminded Sil she still had a job to do.

She looked back at the flitterkin, ready to prod her godlet into action again. Onespot met her gaze.

A spark of kinship flashed between them, just the merest hint of chaos.

Sil sat back on the bed, resisting the urge to sit on her hands like a guilty child. She glanced around to make sure nobody had noticed, but the other bearers of the older gods were intent on their own tasks.

She was supposed to have just invited the older god to extend its protection. But Sil had invited chaos to stay in the flitterkin, and chaos had agreed.

"Oops."

PART V

few seconds later, the lights on the column of equipment flickered out, and Pal lapsed into silence. The others emerged from their reveries and looked around.

Pyr smiled. "We did it."

Mer was the first to notice the new development. "Silver, what did you do?" For once, Mer didn't drag out the syllables of her name.

Sil had been sitting on the bed, relaxing against Crumble's chest, and listening to the steady sound of his heart beating. At Mer's words, she leaned forward so Crumble could turn to look at the flitterkin. "Ha! I might have known." He turned back and pulled her into place again. "That solves one problem, I guess."

Pyr looked from the flitterkin, to Sil, then back to the flitterkin. He slowly shook his head.

Pal just sounded confused and exhausted. "What? What happened?"

"Silver decided to throw out the plan. As usual," Mer said, acid in her voice. "This doesn't solve any problems. It just expands the field."

"I kept the Uncaring God away, didn't I?"

Pal rubbed her face with her free hand. "Would someone please tell me what is going on?"

Crumble angled his head so he could see Pal without moving his torso. "Sil was more successful than the rest of us." He considered a moment. "Or maybe twisted paths sees something in them the other godlets don't." When Pal still looked confused, Crumble gestured with his chin. "Chaos claimed one for its own."

Pal looked at the cage, then took a quick breath. "That's not... I thought they only infected... *inhabited* humans."

Crumble's lips twitched at her correction.

Mer grunted. "*That* was before Silver got involved."

"I don't see how this is my fault. I was supposed to convince it to move into the flitterkin, and I did. How was I supposed to know it would like it there?"

Pyr shook his head. "Clarity had no interest."

"Luck either." Crumble cocked his head and his eyes unfocused. A crease formed on his brow. "They lost the other synthskin..."

Before Mer could respond, there was a gust of cold air as the door opened. Pearl came in, followed by Em. She ignored everyone and strode over to the tower of electronics, stabbing at the displays with one finger. "See! It worked! It was here, and it manifested nearly completely for twenty-three seconds, which should have given it more than enough time to jump to the creatures." She let her arms fall to her sides. "So why didn't it? From Glory's calculations, anything over fourteen seconds should have been enough."

Sil remembered holding the entire universe within her. Twenty-three seconds. When it happened, time had stopped completely.

Crumble bumped her shoulder with his. "Everything okay?"

The memory of the universe fled, leaving room for her to take a breath. "Yes."

At the front of the room, Pearl was still trying to figure out what had gone wrong. "It's as if it didn't even try. But we know it has made an attempt to move into these creatures in the past and just didn't have enough time. So what changed?"

Em gestured at the ceiling with the shotgun. "Most of them are flying around outside, that's what changed."

"It only needs one. And there were four well within the radius." Pearl frowned at Sarge. A chunk of bluequince flew through the air, but the angle of the cage gave Pearl protection from the assault.

Em swung the shotgun toward the rest of the room. "Then it's something they did. I told you keeping Mercury around was a bad idea. And someone's going to be looking for the governor." He scowled at the flitterkin. "Keep the low clan, though. We're going to need them now. I'm not cleaning up after these things."

Mer huffed a laugh. "Do the others know you're planning to replace them yet?" Something in Em's expression answered her question. "Oh, they figured it out, did they? And they left while you were busy elsewhere. So you figure one group of low clan is just as good as another, right? And how do you expect to motivate them without false promises of a payout at the end of it all?"

Em frowned. "They'll work if they want to eat."

Sil looked at Crumble. "Not for that rehydrated stew, I won't." Allowing them to split the group would be disastrous. Besides, Crumble wasn't low clan. She definitely wasn't going to let him go. If Gan and the others had really left, Sil's odds in a fight had greatly improved. They just needed to get loose first.

Pearl frowned at the displays again, then looked sour. "Come on. I need to talk to Glory."

Sil watched them leave. "Did we have a backup to the backup plan?"

Mer shifted so she could look at Pal. "Did you reach someone, or was that mumbling I heard just wishful thinking?"

"I... I *think* I reached someone. They were... No. *He* was asking questions. I tried to make sure I told him everything you wanted me to, but..." She swallowed. "The One God doesn't leave a lot of room for anyone else. I'm not sure how much got through."

Mer sighed. "At least you didn't just add further complications. Any idea of when help might arrive?"

Pal pushed her hair out of her face. "I'm not even sure he's sending help. He spent most of the time asking questions about who I was."

Mer took a breath and let it out slowly. Her face was tight when she turned to face Crumble. "You're still our best bet for getting a message out, especially if they've lost the other synthskin. The instant you have an opening, run."

Outside the window, grey clouds covered the sky, just visible in the fading light. Sil shook her head. "Three days, no supplies, and with a snowstorm blowing through? We have a better chance if we stay here and fight."

"Silver, Pearl has her moments, but she's not that stupid," Mer said. "She's careful. She's not going to let more than one of us free at a time. Even if they've lost the second synthskin, they still outnumber us, and they still have at least one shotgun."

The door opened again, and the humanoid synthskin entered. Sil's stomach sank.

Glory of the Universe must have meant something else when it told Crumble the other synthskin had disappeared. Maybe proximity to the Uncaring God had unbalanced it, or caused communication failures. She tensed, waiting to see who else came through the door. If Pearl figured out what had happened, Sil and Onespot were not going to live long.

But nobody followed the humanoid form through the door. It came over and gripped the band that restrained Crumble. The thread of synthskin drooped, and then flowed into the humanoid's palm, leaving Crumble untethered. Crumble slid out from behind Sil, and knelt in front of her. "May I?" He gestured toward her prosthesis. At her nod, he retrieved the small tools he'd hidden under the bandage and stood up.

"Guard the door," he said quietly.

Sil blinked, not understanding. She was still tethered to the frame of the sleeping pod. Only when the synthskin form headed back to the door did she figure it out.

It was Stuck in the Mud's synthskin in the room with them.

After Mud had been moved off the farm and had access to the network again, it could give the synthskin any configuration it wanted to. It kept the horse form, just as someone might put their own lesser artwork on the wall instead of a copy of a master. But the humanoid form was one of the standard templates. Any humans watching wouldn't be able to tell the difference.

Of course, any humans watching remotely were going to notice that Crumble was moving around. Crumble was only going to have a few minutes, at most, before someone showed up. He passed the equipment tower, opened the closest window, and went to the cages.

"Leave them," Mer said, yanking at the band that held her arm. "We'll have time to euthanize them later. Work on the electronics. If they had a duplicate of the prototype, this wouldn't be the only camp."

Crumble ignored her. He inserted two tools into the lock on the first cage door and closed his eyes.

Mer sounded furious. "We *cannot* allow those things to get loose. We'll never be safe if even one is alive."

Mer was right -- the flitterkin were a threat to everyone's safety. If the Uncaring God could use them as its vessels, keeping them alive left an unbarred door anyone could exploit. The most logical thing to do was kill them. But Crumble was on the other side of the room, and nobody could stop him. Sil wasn't sure she wanted to.

But there was no way he would have time to get all the cages open before the conspirators got past Mud's synthskin. And even if he did, the creatures might still be recaptured before they figured out how to fly. The next time the AIs' god arrived, the older gods wouldn't be here to protect any flitterkin who remained.

So Sil did the only thing she could.

She grabbed her chaos. At least this time, she had some idea of what she was trying to do. She skipped the preliminary fighting with her own godlet and reached for Skinny. *Mine.*

The flitterkin froze, then tilted. For a moment, Sil thought it was going to fall over. Maybe it wasn't strong enough to hold the godlet. Then its eyes widened and it screeched.

Two down, two to go. Sil moved on to Bruiser, but her eyes wouldn't focus. The familiar headache loomed. Of all the inconvenient times for her brain to need sleep... Sil bit her lip, hoping the pain would concentrate her thoughts, but she still couldn't see the flitterkin clearly.

She dug her nails into her palms. "Pyr, I need your medkit."

Without hesitation, Pyr pulled a pouch from his mobility assist. He lobbed it across the room, where it landed between Sil and Pal. Sil upended it on the mattress, sighing in relief when she saw its contents. Pyr had a soldier's understanding of what might be needed in an emergency, including stimulants. She ripped open the packaging of the auto-injector with her teeth and slapped it on the side of her neck.

Her vision opened up, and she could feel the blood pounding in her veins. When this wore off, she'd be weak and shaky. Until then, she would be able to conquer the world.

Crumble yanked at the lock he'd been working on and it fell to the ground. When he opened the cage door, Onespot climbed forward. It ignored the open window and waited on the outside of Skinny's cage. Crumble moved to the next lock.

The blast of a shotgun by the door made Sil jump, but she locked in on Bruiser, grabbed her chaos, and shoved it at the flitterkin. Instead of following her direction, the cat gave an irritated swipe.

A section of the roof overhead caved in, dumping snow and chunks of instacrete on the floor in front of her. Pal screamed and clapped a hand over her mouth.

Too late, Sil remembered the other side effect of the stimulants -- overconfidence. She took a steadying breath, ignored the noises by the door, and imagined stroking the cat lightly. The building tilted. Another shotgun blast rang through the air, the ruined door no longer muffling the noise. But this time when Sil looked at Bruiser, the cat responded. *Mine.*

Bruiser stiffened. Then it let out a screech that echoed through the ruined building.

Sil blew out a breath. Three down, one to go. But the edges of her vision were going grey again. The fight with her godlet had taken too much out of her.

Another shotgun blast. When she looked, Mud's humanoid synthskin was falling backward, half its head missing. The horse form had its important parts protected in the chest, but the humanoid template followed a different pattern.

She *had* to conscript that last flitterkin.

"I need another one." Sil forced herself to form the words carefully, aware that time was skipping forward. She patted around on the bed.

Pal made a noise. Sil had to replay the sound in her head to untangle the words. "Is that safe?"

"No." There were rules about it, and some of the people who ignored those rules died, their hearts spasming into an erratic beat that pumped no blood. "No choice." The grey edges of her vision closed in, no matter how hard she tried to claw her way back. She couldn't find the other injector.

Everything faded away.

---

*P*ain lanced through Sil's chest, making her gasp and feel for the wound that must be there, but her hands only met her undamaged coat. She opened her eyes and saw Pal staring down at her.

"I have about twenty years of grudges to settle, so don't you die on me," Pal said, helping Sil sit up as much as she could while still tethered to the opposite support post. She glanced over her shoulder at the doorway, where Em struggled to reload the shotgun without taking his gloves off. "But the One God agrees this is more important right now."

Sil could see the molecules in the air vibrate. She forced herself to ignore that and sought out the cage where the last flitterkin waited. Crumble had just unlocked the second cage. Onespot and Skinny launched themselves through the window, uncoordinated flapping making them drop sharply out of sight. She hoped they figured out how to fly before anyone found them.

Crumble started on the third lock. Something about his coat had changed. The shoulder was shredded, with the inner lining exposed. Blood dripped slowly down his arm.

Part of her knew he would be fine as long as he got medical attention. He was still upright, using the arm, and didn't seem in any danger of bleeding to death.

The rest of her only saw that Crumble was hurt. She tried to switch her focus over to Sarge. The conspiracy only needed one flitterkin to manifest the Uncaring God permanently. If Em and Pearl stopped Crumble from releasing Sarge, they would have won. Sil wrenched her thoughts onto the flitterkin. *Mine.*

But even as she directed her godlet, she felt her focus drift to Crumble. He was hers, too, in a way. The Uncaring God wasn't *allowed* to hurt him. She felt chaos crash into his luck godlet and braced for the inevitable fight, but luck merely redirected chaos over to the flitterkin. Directing this for the fourth time, Sil felt when chaos settled. Sarge froze, eyes wide, staring at the door.

Sil glanced in that direction. Em raised the shotgun, aiming at Crumble. Sil leaped toward him. The restraint on her wrist yanked her into a different trajectory. She fell to the floor.

There was a blast from the shotgun. A man screamed.

———

SIL HAULED HERSELF OFF THE FLOOR JUST IN TIME TO SEE Sarge leap out the window to the accompaniment of raucous calls and screeches from the flitterkin outside.

Over by the door, twisted metal that had been a shotgun lay on the unmoving synthskin. Em held what remained of his left hand by the wrist. Sil estimated a few minutes before he passed out from blood loss, but in any case, he was no longer an immediate threat.

But Em wasn't the only one out there, and they had at least one more shotgun. Sil's face was wet with sweat. Her heart occasionally skipped a beat, which she thought might have concerned her more at another time. If they could just get free of their restraints, they could leave while the conspirators were distracted by Em's injury. "We need to get these things off," she said to Pal.

"Do you *think* I haven't been..." Pal trailed off and she picked her feet up from the floor. "What is that?"

A crab no bigger than her boot scuttled by, its skin and carapace the grey of synthskin under a layer of muddy clay. Behind it came another thing, with a body as big as her forearm and too many legs to count. A parallelogram of a similar size swooped through the window and crashed into the far wall.

"I... I have no idea." Hallucinations weren't one of the symptoms of stimulant overuse. A second form, rounder than the first, came through the window and bounced off the ceiling onto the floor. Another crab, smaller and a little different from the first, ran in the door. Em's screaming took on a note of disbelief.

All of the synthskin creatures converged on the tower of electronics. A tiny horse climbed through the window, its legs moving in ways a real horse had never moved, but this, at least, she understood. "I'm pretty sure that's Stuck in the Mud's synthskin." Her guess was confirmed when the miniature horse trotted over to stand on the fallen humanoid. The horse grew in size as the form on the floor melted away. Em drew another breath to scream, and then his eyes rolled up and he collapsed.

Two more tiny horses came through the window. Sil shook her head. "Wait, no, I don't know what's going on."

But then Crumble was in front of her, holding one of the tiny horses up to her binding. "I think now would be a good time to leave," he said. Sil's arm came free, and the horse's legs got a bit longer.

She grabbed at the medical supplies strewn around the mattress. "How bad is your shoulder?"

"It can wait." He carried the horse over to Pal and freed her.

The little synthskin forms that weren't horses had disconnected the top box on the tower. It crashed onto the floor and was borne off by a crab. By the time Sil had shoved all the unused medical supplies back in the pouch, the crab had carried its prize out the door. Yells of surprise and anger were quickly followed by cries of pain and then the blast of a shotgun.

Pyr and Mer were already free. Pyr looked a little wildly at the horse that had taken his binding. Mer seemed as unflappable as ever, but she moved slowly, as if it hurt to walk.

Another box from the tower fell to the floor and was carried off.

Sil stood up. The edges of her vision went grey. She wavered and people on both sides grabbed her arms to steady her.

Pal spoke into her ear. "I am *not* carrying you out of here, so don't you dare fall over."

Sil gulped a breath and gestured assent as they all moved toward the door and waited, peeking around the protective bulk of the large synthskin horse. "How are we getting past the people waiting out there?" Most of the conspirators appeared to be either fighting or running from the little synthskin creatures, but there was at least one person with a working shotgun outside.

Mer's voice held its usual acidic tone. "We thought we'd try this one without extra explosions. You just work on keeping up."

"The day I can't outrun the high clan..." Sil muttered.

Another piece of the electronics tower was carried out the door in front of them.

Pyr spoke from the back of the group. "If we get separated, meet up at the tallest cedar over there." Sil followed his finger. The suggestion of a tree was visible through the falling snow. On a good day it would be half an hour's jog from where they stood. On this day, she wasn't sure she could make it at all.

Crumble laid a hand on the large horse. "Ready."

The horse took off downhill at a run, aiming for the person holding the shotgun. Where an actual horse would have needed to navigate carefully in order to avoid a broken leg, the synthskin's limbs scrambled more like a spider.

Pyr made a noise in the back of his throat. "That is just so wrong."

Two blasts of the shotgun didn't slow the synthskin, though what Sil could see of the head didn't look like it was in great shape. Angry yelling turned to cries of panic, and then the horse stopped and settled its bulk on something.

"Time to go," Mer said. She hobbled outside, and stood to the side as the others passed.

Sil exchanged a look with Crumble. He kissed her temple. "Keep your sister safe." He dropped back. Sil heard Mer swear, and then Crumble was scrambling down the slope, Mer held over one shoulder. On areas with icy footing, he slid to stay upright. Sil assumed he was leaning heavily on his luck.

Pyr was next, his mobility assist helping him balance. Sil gave him a few seconds to get in front of them before she pulled Pal along with her. The ground was behaving strangely, at times seeming higher than it looked, and other times making her drop with a jolt. That was the drugs; they were messing with her ability to focus. She just needed to keep it together long enough to get past the conspirators without them noticing --

Sil didn't know who was more surprised, herself or the man with a knife. He had been moving sideways after Pyr and hadn't seen her at all. In her shock, Sil froze, slipped on a patch of ice, and barreled through his shins. He flopped forward, and when Sil stood up and looked back, she saw Pal kick him in the face as she passed.

"We'll make a soldier out of you yet," Sil panted as they hurried after Pyr.

"In your dreams."

On the right side of the line they were traveling, a small ball of synthskin rolled down the hill and opened up to a crab shape when it hit level ground. On the left, a whole group of smaller forms carried the AI core into a gully. Sil ignored them and tried to keep upright. Crumble was somewhere in front of Pyr, and that was the direction they needed to keep heading.

Behind her the shotgun went off again, peppering the dirt to their left. Sil's heart skipped a beat, then two, and she missed a step and ran into a tree trunk. Her heart stuttered to life again. She threw herself forward after Pal. They just needed to get down the hill.

Then the ground leveled off, and Sil and Pal were safely within the cover of the trees.

*I*n the dark of the night, with only the light of the stars to guide them, the quiet surroundings were peaceful. Or, at least, they should have been.

"Are you sure we're going the right way?" Pal's attempt to whisper had been thwarted when she tripped and expelled the final word at a normal volume.

Sil didn't have the energy to sigh. She'd been forced to guide them in a wide arc to avoid the path of the synthskin forms and their stolen electronics. The clouds had broken up after they'd been walking for a while, making navigation more reliable, but if her calculations had been wrong in that first hour, they could be far from where she thought they were.

She knew they had only been walking for a few hours, but it was starting to feel like they'd been there for days. Sil was exhausted, but afraid to stop for rest in case she fell asleep and froze to death.

On the positive side, her heart had settled into a steady rhythm, and her sense of time had leveled out after the drugs had worn off. She was pretty sure she wasn't going to become a cautionary tale about ignoring the warnings on the stimulant packages. That might not matter, though, if she spent the rest of her life locked up for murdering her sister. The woman would not shut up.

She paused and pulled Pal's head close to hers, both so she could speak quietly and also point up to the sky. "Those two bright stars are in a line running north-south. The colony is over there." She waved to their right. "And the tree we're meeting at is over there." She gestured in front of them. "More or less."

Pal's face was just visible in the night. "What do you mean 'more or less'?"

"I haven't done this sort of thing in a while. I could have messed up the distances." With the damaged prosthesis, her stride length was neither even nor consistent, and her compensation for that had been a gamble. "We should be in the right area, though. I hope."

Pal pulled away. "If I had just left when I had wanted to, I'd be back home with my wife by now, not freezing on One God blighted Jackpot Drift." But her complaint held no anger -- it just seemed to be a statement of fact.

"Probably," Sil agreed. "But you might have still been in the wormhole when they succeeded in manifesting their god." She started walking again.

"At least I would have died with a full stomach and a comfortable bed."

"Now you really do sound like a soldier."

Pyr's voice broke in from their left. "It's about time you two showed up."

Pal blew out a breath. "Oh, thank the One God."

Sil tried not to be insulted by the relief in her sister's voice as they walked toward Pyr. "Crumble and Mer?"

"Already here. She's patching him up."

"Not you?" Sil tripped over a tree root and caught herself.

Pyr had always been in charge of treating minor wounds at the Bog & Bellow.

"Somebody had to keep an eye out so you two didn't walk right by. Besides, Mer's pretty handy at field medicine. Hidden depths, our Mer."

Sil suspected Mer had a five story building complete with a topiary garden hidden in her depths. Her ability to do rudimentary first aid didn't surprise Sil. They wound among a thick grove of trees, and then suddenly there was a shielded light ahead. Crumble was grinning and speaking quietly as a blank-faced Mer bandaged his upper arm. Just seeing his face let Sil take a deeper breath. He looked up then and smiled at her.

She waited until Pal had moved ahead. "Thanks. We would have kept walking. I thought we were further south."

"Not a problem. It gave me an excuse to get away from the clash of the unstoppably cheerful and immovably grim."

Sil smiled at that image. Then she sobered. "We're in all levels of trouble out here. No food, no way to filter water." Of all of them, she was least likely to be affected by that last, having already been exposed to most of the pathogens in the local water. "No source of heat. Plus, I'm going to collapse at some point soon and then I may be out for a long while."

"And I have about half a day before my power is out and I'm stuck using my arms to move forward," Pyr added. "But we do have a little food. The... horse-thing showed up a little while ago and dropped off some rations."

Sil sighed.

Pyr huffed a laugh. "Yeah. Then it spit out another med kit and disappeared again. I'm hoping it comes back with tents and a blanket, but that's probably too much to ask."

"Why not a portable hot tub?"

"I'm not sure I could endure that small a space with your man and Mer."

"Point."

"I figure we should rest here for the night and start toward town in the morning, those of us who can move anyhow."

Splitting the group didn't seem like a great idea, but Sil didn't see how they could avoid it. That was a problem for the morning, though. First, she needed to get some sleep.

———

WHEN SIL WOKE, THE GREY LIGHT OF DAWN WAS FILTERING through the trees. The whole group was huddled together for warmth, and Crumble had pulled branches over them, both to hold the heat and to hide them from searchers. Pal's quiet snores were almost comforting.

Somehow Sil was unsurprised to find the goat had shoved her way between Sil and Mer and was now munching on the greenery. That cemented things -- this was Captain Idiot's daughter, Sil was sure of it now. She reached up to scratch the goat's forehead.

Mer's voice came from the other side of the goat. "Do all the low clan attract farm animals wherever they go, Silver, or is that your specialty?"

"Jealous, Mer?"

"I've had worse bedmates." There was a moment of quiet. "They're going to be waiting for you at the southern entrance to town. You and the Oldlander need to take the governor the long way around and enter from the north."

If it had been a matter of just getting a message through and sending help, Mer wouldn't have included Pal. But it was winter. Taking the long way would add at least two or three days to their journey. Even if a storm didn't delay rescuers, Mer and Pyr would have been without shelter or supplies for a week. Those conditions were survivable in summer, but not during winter on Jackpot Drift.

"We'll go back this morning and steal a vehicle," Sil countered. "They can't try to manifest the god again until they capture some flitterkin and get their equipment back..." She stopped. She'd been too tired to even try to figure things out the night before. "Sorry, I'm feeling a little slow this morning. Exactly *where* did all those synthskin things come from?"

Mer made a sound that might have been a grunt or a laugh. "No idea. I thought maybe chaos was involved."

"I don't think so." Crumble had once told her that bringing chaos too close to an AI caused *spectacular* results, but she didn't think he had been referring to an army of miniature synthskin animals. "Anyhow, there's no need to rush to get a message through. Someone has to be looking for Pal by now. We just need to stay put and get found by the right people."

"And how do you propose we do that?"

Crumble's voice was rough from sleep. "The Zoom Zoom Room just broadcast from orbit. It's sending down a shuttle with fliers to search for us."

Mer's voice was flat. "That's the ship that brought the hala trees. It won't be here to help us."

"I did it a favor when it was in orbit before. It *might* be here to help us."

Sil leaned back against him. "Best guess -- friend or foe?"

"Friend."

Sil yawned. "Good enough for me. Can you contact it?"

"Only when one of the fliers gets close enough."

"Then I'm going back to sleep for a while. Nobody tell Pal, though. I want to see the look on her face when she finds out she has to go up in the bucket."

———

Hours later, Sil woke with a hand over her mouth. Crumble whispered in her ear. "Flier's crew is looking for a spot to set down, but we have people nearby."

Sil tapped the hand over her mouth in acknowledgement, and he released her. She sat up slowly and looked around. Pal huddled in the space between two trees, arms wrapped around her legs, shivering so much Sil thought it unlikely she'd be able to move on her own. Mer and Pyr were standing at opposite ends of the clearing, stout branches in hand. The goat stripped bark off a tree, unconcerned with what the rest of them were doing.

Sil let Crumble help her to her feet and found her newest problem. Either from the cold or the abuse, her prosthesis had locked up. It would help her stand, but she would have to use leverage and momentum to walk with it. If they had to travel quickly, she was in trouble. She took the stick Crumble handed her and used it as a crutch to move so her back was against a tree.

They didn't have long to wait.

Pearl walked confidently forward, Em stomping along behind her, one hand encased in a huge bandage. This time Pearl had the shotgun. "Ah, there you are! I was hoping we wouldn't have to keep looking during the storm that's coming. It's never safe to just assume someone died. I always like to have confirmation."

Mer shifted to put most of her weight on one leg. "Looks like I missed at least one person in town." She caught Sil's eye and gestured toward Pal with her chin. "Even with her tracker activated, they wouldn't be able to locate her without the right sequence. Someone back in town is feeding them information." She cocked her head and looked at Pearl. "Or maybe more than information. Are they going to give you a place to stay for the winter, or are you just waiting to be picked up by another ship that can go through the gate?

Another colony might not be isolated enough for what you're doing."

"Not something you need to worry about, Mer." Pearl looked at everyone in the clearing. "I only need a couple of you to serve as bait for the god, and I think we've learned our lesson about keeping *all* of you around. So the question is, who gets to come with me, and who gets to feed the trees?" She raised the shotgun and swung it around the clearing. When she stopped, the muzzle pointed at Crumble. "How can you stand to be around an Oldlander?"

Sil's stomach clenched. Pearl was too far away for anyone to reach her in time. Worse, Crumble was paying attention to something only he could hear. Ridiculous. *This* was why nobody took mechs out in the field. They got distracted and forgot to duck.

She forced herself to keep her voice light. "The last time someone tried to fire one of those things around us, it blew up." She raised her eyebrows at Em. "How's the hand?" She poked her godlet, hoping it might bring down a branch or even a small tree, but with the three other gods nearby, it merely purred and rolled over.

A crackle from the bushes caught Pearl's attention, and she wheeled around. But it was only the goat stripping a branch of bark and leaves. Pearl turned back and pointed the shotgun at Crumble again.

Even if the Zoom Zoom Room's crew were in the area, they weren't going to get here in time. Sil gave up on waiting. Using her good leg and the branch, she threw herself forward, turning as she fell, and landing on her back. She brought the stick around with a two-handed swing that skimmed just over the ground.

In her mind, the arc of her swing would have ended at Pearl's legs. But her leap hadn't been far enough, and the stick was too short, so there was just a whistle of wind as the end of the stick kept moving.

Pearl looked down at her untouched shins and then at Sil. "That might have hurt. But I guess we have our second volunteer for tree feeding." Her finger moved over the trigger.

A huge metal wrench arced through the air into the back of Pearl's head, knocking her forward a step. She staggered, righted herself, and turned -- just in time for Ore, the flier's winch operator, to drop out of the tree and wrest the shotgun away. He tossed it out of reach and immobilized Pearl by grabbing the collar of her coat and straightening his arm.

Behind them, the goat lowered her head and rammed into Em. Two other people wearing coats with the hala logo grabbed him as he stumbled and fell.

The winch operator looked at Crumble and smiled. "Zoom said we had to come back to keep you safe. But if you think you're going to trick me into another card game... Well, we'll have to see about that."

Crumble smiled back as he helped Sil to her feet. "I'm sure you'll make the right decision."

That made all three of the tree planters laugh. The winch operator glanced at the sky. "Zoom says there's a nasty storm coming in. How about we take this discussion to someplace warmer?"

*B*etween getting everyone back to town, and
tracking down the doctor so she could look at
Crumble's shoulder, and then taking time to finally get clean,
it was fully dark by the time they all gathered in the dining
room at the house.

The Zoom Zoom Room and its crew had headed back
through the gate as soon as they'd dropped everyone off, as
the AI had realized if they didn't leave immediately, the ship
would likely be stuck there for a while. It had a split to
perform back at Platinum Sun Station and it couldn't take
the risk of further instability while parked in orbit around
Jackpot Drift.

Crumble and the winch operator had made plans for a
rematch the next time the Zoom Zoom Room was in the
system.

After the doctor had finished with Crumble, Sil had given
her what remained of the prosthesis. The doctor had stared
at it in disbelief, and then left the house without another
word.

Now Sil sat at the table, stomach comfortably full, letting

the conversation flow over her as she kept an ear out for signs of trouble from the goats. Captain Idiot's daughter had come back with them -- Sil couldn't leave a goat alone out there, no matter what anyone said.

Bringing the doe along had even been helpful -- after Sil had pointed out the goat had gone up to the flier without complaining, Pal set her jaw and stepped into the bucket. Sil had barely been able to hear Pal's clenched-jaw keening over the sound of the wind.

Across the table, Mer set her mug down. "We need to decide what to do."

Sil pulled her attention back to the room. This was new. Until now, Mer had always done whatever it was she did, working out who needed to be questioned further, and arranging for that to happen. Now Pearl and Em were in stasis boxes locked in the post office. Sil had assumed she would never hear anything about them again.

Pal frowned. "What needs to be decided? We have the people in charge. All their equipment is gone. We don't need to worry about anyone manifesting the Uncaring God anymore." She took a deep breath and let it out. "And against my better judgment, I've decided not to say anything about the older gods that seem to be all over the place." She grimaced. "Since the One God seems not to mind."

Sil snorted. "Nice of it to overlook that after not lifting a finger to help for so long."

Mer cut in before Pal could respond. "Four of the flitterkin are protected, but the others aren't. If they all freeze or starve this winter, one of our problems will be solved, but I don't think we can count on that. I assume the eventual goal when they were created was to release them on the planet, to allow the god to manifest at will. They can't be as fragile as all that."

Pyr raised one eyebrow. "If they can survive on the planet,

they may not be confined to this valley. We'll never be able to track them all down."

Mer gave a sharp gesture of assent. "The other approach is to follow the AIs. We know where Glory of the Universe is housed, though I suspect it will either be gone or have wiped itself by the time we get back there. But there was another AI helping. I have suspicions of which one it might be, but I still don't have any proof."

Pyr spoke while he topped up their mugs with more tea. "And you're telling this to us, why?" He kept pouring while he met her gaze. "Forgive me for pointing out a painful truth, but I'm fairly sure I'm the closest thing you have to either a friend or colleague in this system. You've been careful not to talk about this before, even to me."

Pal straightened in her chair. "As governor, I..." She trailed off as they all looked at her. "Relax. That was supposed to be a joke."

Crumble leaned over to murmur in Sil's ear. "I think I'm starting to like your sister."

"I suppose somebody should."

"Things at the agency are..." Mer paused, as if searching for the right word. "Things are *unsettled*. I've been assured that changes have been made, are being made even now, but at this point only a fool would trust them." She stared at Pyr. "And there is too much at stake to allow myself to be a fool."

Pyr folded his hands on the table. "You spoke of decisions."

"Yes. I suspect if we can't show evidence that we've contained this conspiracy, Jackpot Drift will be named as the problem itself."

Pyr cocked his head, communicating with the godlet of clarity only he could hear. "At least some faction will consider sterilizing the planet to be the best solution."

Sil glanced around the table. The only person who

showed any real surprise was Pal. The governor frowned. "Evacuating and resettling the planet would take *enormous* resources." She stopped talking when nobody tried to argue. "You don't think they would evacuate? But surely..."

Mer shrugged. "As you say, it would require resources. And there is always the possibility evacuees will transfer the contagion to a different place, one that might not be so disposable."

"But..."

Pyr reached over to touch Pal's arm. "We're not saying it's the only choice, or even one that anyone is likely to agree to. But it's a possibility we need to be prepared for." He took his hand from her arm and raised his mug. "That means we need to be prepared if the gate goes down."

Mer cocked her head. "That means we need to be prepared to *take* the gate down."

"The AIs may be willing to help you with that," Crumble said. He looked directly at Mer. "The flitterkin are a new, sentient species, only found on Jackpot Drift. The AIs will stop an extinction event if they can."

Mer narrowed her eyes at him. "If you're waiting for me to say I was wrong in planning to euthanize them all, you're going to be waiting until the universe collapses."

Pyr cut in before Crumble could respond. "Regardless of past intentions, the flitterkin are loose now. Will the AIs help block the gate if we need them to? They seemed upset the last time it was down."

The AIs had gone on strike the last time the gate had stopped transmitting information. Sil couldn't imagine what would happen in the colony if the AIs refused to help at all.

"I'll talk to them." Crumble tapped the table. "It would certainly be less destructive than stealing a ship and messing with the wormhole stabilizing hardware."

The quiet click of hooves on tile came from the hallway

leading to the bedroom suites. Sil fought the urge to bury her head in her hands and grabbed her crutches. "I need to check the bedroom door."

It was bad enough Captain Idiot had learned to open the doors when the weather had been warmer. Now the temperatures had dropped, and the goat hadn't yet started closing the door behind her. Built for a different climate to begin with, this house was going to have snow piling up in the hallway if they weren't careful.

But it wasn't Captain Idiot she found nibbling on the decorative screen at the opening of the reception hallway. It was Captain Idiot's daughter. "Outside." Sil nudged the goat with one crutch and followed her back down the hall to her bedroom. As expected, the door leading outside was wide open, freezing air blowing in. "You made it through the winter so far on your own up in the hills, and it's warmer down here. You can stay outside."

She almost didn't notice Captain Idiot lying on the bed. Eventually she got both goats outside, closed the door, and locked it again. They still hadn't figured out how the goats were getting in.

When she got back to the table, Crumble had broken out the wine. "Everything okay?" he asked as he handed her a glass with just a bit.

"They've started working together." She tipped the contents into her mouth and swirled them around. Someone had been experimenting with a bluequince citrus mix, not entirely successfully. "This might need a little more aging."

Pyr disagreed. "If you wait another two weeks it's going to turn."

Pal sniffed and set the glass down. "That's awful."

"You get used to it." Mer held her glass out for Crumble to fill. "If we're going to have the gates going down, we'll have to really work on the colony's self-sufficiency."

Sil let them carry on with the familiar arguments and held out her glass for Crumble to pour more wine into. "I haven't fallen asleep yet today." She knew he had noticed, but he would never say anything unless she brought it up first.

He smiled. "Progress, indeed."

"But I don't think the doctor is going to graft on the new leg quite yet. And she wasn't very happy with the state of the prosthesis she gave me a few days ago."

Crumble buried his grin by taking another sip of wine. "What do you think about a goat cart?"

"I think if I get into a cart pulled by either of those goats, it will be the last you ever see of me." She scooted her chair closer and leaned against him as she listened to the other three hashing out their priorities. "If we have a governor who is working for the colony, that could make a big difference." She sighed. "Even if she is my sister."

"Admit it. She's growing on you, too."

Perhaps. But they still needed to convince Pal to stay.

*J*ackpot Drift, Private Communication:

> *Speed of Violet Thoughts*: Good news! The forms have started coming in.

Scary Not Scary: I thought we decided the best outcome was if they all disappeared forever.

Speed of Violet Thoughts: This is better. They're bringing in the hardware used by the god-bringers. Plus, the horse form is with them, so everyone will think they belong to *Stuck in the Mud*.

Scary Not Scary: I'm pretty sure *Stuck in the Mud* is the reason they all went off course in the first place.

Speed of Violet Thoughts: I think so, too. Still, it helped bring our favorite mech back, so I guess we can forgive it for absorbing the leaders and messing up the entire competition. We've probably lost some of the synthskin permanently, but not much.

Scary Not Scary: I suppose we could ask for it back, but...

Speed of Violet Thoughts: Right. It's a small price to pay for making it look like this was all *Stuck in the Mud*'s doing.

Scary Not Scary: And since nobody other than our favorite mech can get any sense out of it...

Speed of Violet Thoughts: We're in the clear.

Scary Not Scary: That *is* good news. I thought we were going to end up in real trouble.

Speed of Violet Thoughts: We definitely should be more careful.

Scary Not Scary: So the next challenge...

Speed of Violet Thoughts: What do you think about a race around the borders of the terraformed section?

Scary Not Scary: Done. And I'm sending some recording devices with mine. I've always wondered what's out there.

Speed of Violet Thoughts: To make it fair, I'll send the same thing with mine. Winner is the first one to get the recording device back to the post office.

Scary Not Scary: Agreed. And if everything goes wrong, we'll just let everyone assume it was *Stuck in the Mud* again.

Speed of Violet Thoughts: Yes. We probably ought to help it find a language module it can work with.

Scary Not Scary: I've sent queries.

Speed of Violet Thoughts: Good. Speaking of queries, what do you know about *Just Passing Through*?

Scary Not Scary: Just what everyone else knows. It has a self-powered vehicle, which I covet, and an obsession with fish, which I do not. Why do you ask?

Speed of Violet Thoughts: I saw a request for data that suggested there isn't a registration in that name.

Scary Not Scary: Probably just an error in the records. Or an unregistered split. You know how that goes.

Speed of Violet Thoughts: Probably. But it's interesting, isn't it?

Scary Not Scary: It was already here when I got in-system. I'll start loading the colony archives and see what I can find.

Speed of Violet Thoughts: I think it would be good to know.

But keep it quiet. I don't like how many AIs have been wiped lately.

Scary Not Scary: Will do.

Speed of Violet Thoughts: Thanks. I'll ping you when the contest starts.

*T*o: Senior Agent Mercury Sweetair, eyes only
Decrypted data follows:

ADDITIONAL INFORMATION NEEDED:

1) Total number of uncontained genetically modified animals (termed "flitterkin" in the most recent report) on Jackpot Drift.

2) List of all ships that have left the system in the past two standard years.

3) Probability of survival of modified animals ("flitterkin") during seasonal shifts on Jackpot Drift.

4) Current census data for Jackpot Drift (human and AI).

5) Any unreported strategic importance of the Jackpot Drift system.

AT THE COMPLETION OF THIS REQUEST FOR INFORMATION, YOU are to transfer to Platinum Sun Station and report to Ruthenium Mountdrop.

---

*B*ack in her workshop two days later, Sil eyed the equipment as she took off her coat and settled her crutches next to her. A thin film of dust covered everything, the only evidence that anything different had happened in the past few days.

If Jackpot Drift was cut off from the rest of the universe, nothing in her workshop would be affected, at least initially. But its importance would skyrocket. If there was no other way to replace broken equipment, her shop would be the single point of failure for any automated process used in the entire colony. They needed redundancy, and they needed it as soon as possible. She started a list.

Ten minutes after Sil had sent the list off to the governor's office, Pal came through the door. "Do you have any idea how expensive this stuff is?"

Sil pulled off her goggles and swiveled to face her sister. "Only vaguely. Not my job. But that's why I gave you a breakdown of what we need depending on how long we're cut off."

Pal's face looked drawn, as if she had a headache, or maybe hadn't been sleeping well. "The ten-year list is blank."

Sil shrugged. "If the gates are down for more than ten years, we're all going to be farming or dead and none of this will matter. How much panic did the inventory cause in the high clan?" The low clan had half-expected to be abandoned for years; the only thing new for them was having a governor who understood it was a possibility.

"Not as much as I thought it would. Everyone is assuming they'll have transferred away before it happens." She tucked a strand of hair behind her ear. "I told my wife I'm staying. At least for a while."

"Ah." That explained the sleepless nights. "And how did she take it?"

"I don't know yet. She hasn't responded. When I first got transferred, we talked about whether she could switch to a cargo run that came here. But it would be a demotion, and I was only planning to stay while they went through the normal process of selecting a new governor. Being separated for a few months, or even a year, didn't seem like a huge disruption."

"But now..." Sil prompted.

"The One God wants me to stay. I *did* reach a priest on Station Prime the other day. I thought I had, but I got confirmation today. He apologized for not sending help earlier. The request needed approval from someone who was out of the office." She huffed a laugh. "Bureaucracy will be the death of us all."

"Not me. I'm planning to die in a bar fight." Sil grabbed her coat. "Speaking of which, do you feel like lunch at the Bog & Bellow?"

Pal paused in the middle of agreeing. "Will that be okay? Since it's low clan and I'm..."

Sil waved off her questions. "Aurum's high clan and he's *working* there, so I think you should be fine. Though they might make you buy a round of drinks for everyone. I'm not sure how that's working. Anyhow, Crumble was baking when I left this morning, and he's bound to have brought something good for Pyr to sell." Crumble was determined to make the bittergreen part of a recipe that was *someone*'s favorite.

They were almost at the door before Sil could force herself to say what she needed to. "I'm sorry you're stuck here. No, sincerely," she added when Pal gave her a suspicious look. "We need someone to stay and advocate for the colony, but being forced into it by the One God isn't fair to you."

Pal opened the door. "Even without the One God... I can't just leave this place and depend on the next person to get it right." She shoved her hands in the pockets of her coat. "It's not so much that I'm great at what I do, but at least I'm here."

"Rho hardly ever bothered to come down from orbit," Sil pointed out. "So already you're the best governor on Jackpot Drift for years." The air was crisp, and the skies promised more snow later in the day.

Pal's laugh barely made it to Sil's ears. "I just wish this place wasn't so horrible."

Sil set a path that would take them around the cobblestones. "Give it some time. It grows on you."

"Everybody keeps telling me that, but I'm not sure any of you believe it."

Sil looked at Pal, who had stopped and was staring at her feet. "You kept the boots."

"Did you think I was going to go through that pile and find something else?" She scraped the sole along the pavement. "I just stepped in a pile of... sheep manure?"

"Mini-cow," Sil corrected. She caught her sister's eye. "It grows on you slowly. Very, very slowly."

———

THEY WERE NEARLY AT THE BOG & BELLOW, DODGING A GOAT cart and a gaggle of children so bundled up they couldn't bend at the waist, when Pal spoke again. "They shouldn't have pressed charges."

Sil glanced up. "For the rooster thing? That was just the only way Glass could figure out how to get me to work for him as a nanotech." She shrugged. "That was how he ran things."

Pal was silent for a few more steps. "I meant back home."

Home meant Jackpot Drift for Sil, so it took her a few seconds to figure out that Pal meant the city they'd grown up in. "Oh. That."

"It wasn't right. You were still a minor, and it was wrong to force you into the army like that." She took a deep breath. "I don't ask for forgiveness, but I might be able to explain the..." She stopped. "What did your Oldlander call it? We talked for a bit about how to understand the One God yesterday. The *context*? Maybe that's it. You thought you were just humiliating my... our father."

"That was the goal," Sil agreed. It had happened half a lifetime ago. Now she couldn't even remember why she'd been so angry.

A harnessed mini-cow trotted past, pulling a child who was standing on some sort of modified skis. A mob of children about the same age ran after them.

"It worked. Everyone who knew him heard about it. More than that," she said, reaching down to steady a child who had bounced off her leg. "They heard about it and knew that it had all come out because of his daughter, who was low clan. That was the part that really got people talking. The whole thing was so embarrassing for all of us."

Stuck in the Mud's horse synthskin rounded the corner, following the mini-cow.

Now Sil was starting to remember why she'd been angry enough to sabotage her entire life just to get back at one person. If Pal kept talking long enough, Sil might consider a follow up.

Pal continued, apparently oblivious. "But it also cracked the foundation of our family. Oh, not that he had been with another woman," she added. "I don't think either of them had any illusions. They married because they had shared goals; it was never meant to be a monogamous love match. But when my mother found out he'd had this whole other relationship, with a child, and he'd been hiding everything about it all those years... It was *that* lie that caused the issue. And once she saw that lie, of course, she saw all the other lies and started questioning everything, including business matters." She shrugged. "They eventually patched it over, but she took it out on him and he took it out on you."

Sil tried to imagine what her life would have been like if she hadn't joined the army. If she'd stayed home, she would have had more time with her mother, which would have been both a blessing and a curse. Even after Sil was old enough to understand they were never going to be raised to high clan, she hadn't known how to let that go. The army had knocked that out of her pretty quickly.

"No, it wasn't right," Sil said after she'd thought about it for a few steps. "But..." She shrugged. "I think I would never have become the person I am today without it." She glanced over at her sister. "I suppose I ought to apologize to you. I meant to harm *him*. Collateral damage never occurred to me."

"I looked up to him. And then I didn't," Pal said simply. "But maybe that's just part of growing up." She paused with her hand on the pub door. "Just because I think what happened was wrong doesn't mean I *like* you, or think of you as family."

Sil couldn't stop the snort of laughter that came out. "Thank the One God. If I had to be nice to you I'd probably explode." She met Pal's eyes and saw her lips twitch. Sil didn't try to keep the grin off her face as they went into the warmth of the bar.

*I*n the dark of the night, clean and dry and warm, Sil woke up to an unfamiliar scratching sound. She elbowed Crumble. The noise came again, but this time she pinpointed it to the ledge of the roof, outside the window. "How did the goats get on the roof?"

Crumble made a noise in the back of his throat. "It's not the goats. It's the flitterkin. This is one of those things I didn't think to warn you about."

Out in the darkness, Sil heard a goat bleat and then settle down again. She waited.

"When there are a few avatars for the same older god in the same place, a quorum is formed. It's the basis for a temple. Not something physical," he added as she raised her head to look out the window. "But it's a call to gather. I wasn't sure if it would apply in this instance, but..."

Sil thought about the colony, and the huge church to the One God in the center. "So now wherever we are, there's a chaos temple?" She couldn't help it. She laughed. "It's very..."

Crumble slid a hand down her back, waking her skin in

the best possible way. "It's very you." His fingers moved up, trailing along her ribs. "We'll figure something out."

Later they would deal with the chaos temple she had created, and the colony's need for self-sufficiency, and what was left of the conspiracy to manifest the Uncaring God, and the unprotected flitterkin, and everything else that needed to happen, including finding and installing goat-proof doors. And raising chickens.

For tonight she would enjoy having a warm bed, and the man beside her. Everything else could wait.

Sil pulled him toward her. "Tomorrow," she said firmly. Tonight, she had other plans.

*P*rivate encrypted communication
To: AI *Speed of Violet Thoughts*
From: Mercury Sweetair

SEE ATTACHED DECRYPTED DATA. ANALYSIS SUGGESTS THEY ARE exploring the possibility of sterilizing Jackpot Drift.

I'VE SENT A REPORT INDICATING THE FLITTERKIN COULD HAVE left the system. That may not delay them for long.

BE READY.

———

I HOPE YOU ENJOYED READING ABOUT JACKPOT DRIFT AS MUCH AS I enjoyed writing it!

If you would like to be notified when the next book is available, as well as receive exclusive short stories, you can sign up for my free newsletter at https://tmbaumgartner.com/subscribe/.

ACKNOWLEDGMENTS

My name might be alone on the cover, but many people helped get this book into its final form.

I owe a huge debt to my fellow writers in the WF critique group — I threw up my hands and gave them the first (horrible) draft, asking them to figure out what was wrong. They told me, and also gave me excellent suggestions on how to fix it.

Writing can be an isolating pastime, but my friends and family are just wonderful people in general. While I'd love to believe it's my influence on them, I know I'm just lucky. You are all awesome!

And finally, thank you to my brother Eric, who did the final check looking for typos and flagrant punctuation errors. It's a good thing that *one* of us paid attention in English class.

ABOUT THE AUTHOR

T. M. Baumgartner is a speculative fiction writer who has difficulty following directions. This probably explains why the IRS recalculates her tax refund after she files it every year. At various times she has been a veterinarian, Unix system administrator, software developer, and after-hours book-shelver in a medical library.

Theresa currently lives in Northern California in a house with too many animals. She knits hats for garden gnomes and fails to grow tomatoes despite living in the perfect climate.

She also writes cozy mysteries under the pen name Tess Baytree.

Want updates about new releases? Silly dog anecdotes? Free stories? Join the newsletter mailing list! Go to https://tmbaumgartner.com/subscribe/ or point your phone's camera at the QR code above.

———

The marketing department here at Speculative Turtle Press is great at tail wagging, but a little challenged by tasks that require thumbs.

If you enjoyed this book and would like to help other readers find it, please tell your friends and consider leaving a review at your favorite site.